LOOPING FOR LOVE

Looping for Love

Ginney Etherton

Copyright © 2011 by Ginney Etherton

ISBN 978-0-9835581-1-8

Cover design by Matthew Hanna
                    matthewhanna@mac.com

For Christo, who keeps me laughing,
and loving

ACKNOWLEDGMENTS

I thank Paulianne Balch for her innate editor's eye, and offer my apologies for all remaining errors; they are entirely due to my willful disregard of the rules. My gratitude also goes to Heidi Connolly for giving me tips on book design, and to Matthew Hanna for getting the cover just right. Thank you to friends: Nanci Johnson for the creative spark that started the whole thing; Rosaria Williams for introducing me to great Italian dining; Shalisa Singleton and Nancy Angelesco for reading unpolished versions and still saying nice things. As always, I thank the talented and fun folks in my writers group for their countless critiques and encouragement. And although he may say differently, my appreciation for all things golf goes to my husband, Christo Schwartz.

Finally, my heartfelt gratitude to Rich and Annie, the "Technical Advisors" who taught me the caddie biz.
Regrettably, due to a tragic accident and an unjust court, I lost them too early and had to muddle through on my own.

CHAPTER 1

"TIDWELL!"

The caddie master's booming voice shook me out of a homicidal fantasy.

"You've got a bag. Head out to the Hollows."

"Thank god. If I had to stay here another minute with these clowns, I might go postal with a 6-iron."

I could feel the boys eyeing me as I walked, and I knew what was coming.

Rocks made sure his voice was heard across the caddie shack. "Yeah, Sweetcheeks. Show us your fine form."

That brought yet another burst of adolescent sniggers from the pack. I'd been there for three hours. That's too long for anyone to be held in close quarters with more than one caddie, let alone a roomful. I'd heard enough stupid jokes and lying brags of sexual exploits to make me gag. It's cruel and unusual punishment, maybe worthy of a Workers' Comp claim.

"Stuff it, Rocks." I pointed a ragged nail in his face. "And the next time I hear you bad-mouthing me to the players like you did yesterday, Larson will have to call a paramedic to get your gonads out of your chest."

This time the laughter was louder.

"Okay, okay, Tidwell. Cool it." Larson, the caddie master, stepped between us. "Rocks, show some class. No one at this club shows disrespect for another crew member. Got it?"

"I was just jokin' around with..."

"Nothing. No jokes, no smart-ass stuff directed at anyone connected to Singing Bluffs in front of the guests. Ever. Now get out of here, Tidwell. Rocks is with the second foursome after yours, so you shouldn't be seeing him again today."

Larson was an alright guy. For a caddie master in charge of over 200 caddies going in and out of here on a daily basis, he usually kept a level head and always treated me fairly. Being the smallest woman of only six or seven on the free-agent squad, I have to take a lot of crap, but never from Larson.

As usual, what had initially seemed like a dream job turned out to be a nightmare in a matter of weeks. But what did I expect? When I drove into this town two years ago with nothing but my dog and what I could carry in my old Jeep hardtop, I wasn't looking for the high life.

I'm Lainey Tidwell, twenty-four, barely five feet tall and cursed with a build like a 49ers cheerleader. My temperament would be better suited to the stump physique of a logger. My dad taught me how to cuss before I was ten, and my mom never could get me to stop burping out loud. So jobs where you're expected to be ladylike just weren't in the cards for me. Waiting tables, checking at the grocery store, even picking shrimp at the fish plant required more sensibilities than I was able to pull off reliably. Landing a job at the new golf course, the only big thing going on in this off-the-beaten-path small town, was right up my alley. I'm an independent contractor, I get to work outdoors, I make huge tips from wealthy golf nuts, and I'm making bold, feminist steps by showing that I can hold my own as a woman in a man's world.

How did I know that most of the men I'd be around would be preppy, wife-cheating assholes and sophomoric, obnoxious losers?

Waiting was the worst. As an unassigned caddie, you get here before six-thirty and then wait for incoming players. If you're lucky and the guy likes you, you get assigned to him for the length of his stay. The key was to earn your way to the A-squad, the seniors, and get your name on the pre-assignment sheet. But to be a senior you have be "in the bucket" for a season, and it didn't hurt, I was told, to kiss the ass of the caddie services manager either.

As far as caddie shacks go, this one was supposedly a five-star. The itinerant caddies tell stories of folding chairs and vending machines in overheated trailers or cold, unfurnished cart barns, so we can't complain. It's roomy, with comfortable furniture and a 32-inch plasma TV. We can order at the window of the clubhouse bar, but the food is limited to greasy fried stuff, and alcoholic drinks are strictly forbidden, of course. Still, if you bring a book it's not a horrible place.

But the company....

When I trained to be on the bag, I was given the impression of a corps of skilled professionals with a passion for the sport, keen instincts to read greens and the elements, and a comedian's talent for making small talk. One of the things we learned in our two night-school sessions at the community college – besides basic knowledge of scoring, standing in the right place, tending the flags, replacing divots, raking bunkers, and the zillion other things we do to give the player a great day on the course – was that caddying has a proud history. There are veterans, men with a code of expertise, who can not only choose clubs and read yardages and putts, they know how to get the feel of the player. They are able to figure the mood, the skill level, the ego of their golfers and make their day.

It sounded a lot like another proud profession – the world's oldest.

Since I wasn't much of an athlete but I *was* good at men, I was excited. This could be my game! I didn't have to *play* it, I just had to *know* it. I was willing to work hard and learn from the pros. But what I wasn't prepared for were the busloads of bag-toters who took the job here just for some fast money. And because Singing Bluffs had its share of super-rich hackers throwing it around, they made a ton.

MY LOOP FINISHED earlier than I expected because the guests were old-timers. The old-timers are the best. Golfers over fifty don't fool around. They usually have a surprisingly fast pace of play because they have more respect for the game, for the course, and, not insignificantly, for me. There was only one other caddie with us, Randy a.k.a. "Hands," who is usually mouthy and crude, which could have ruined my day. But he was double-bagging and too occupied with his guys' bunker

4

shots to pay attention to me. The one player who packed his own bag was a head pro from some fancy-schmancy course in So-Cal who tried to give my old duffer some pointers, so I kept quiet most of the time. I told them the yardages to the greens and flagsticks, and pointed out the false calms behind the dunes that lulled first-timers to the course into pulling the wrong club. Some polite chit-chat along with the basic caddie services and I'd earned my $50 caddie fee plus a fair $50 tip. All in all, I couldn't have asked for a more gentlemanly group.

Which is why I ended the day back in town at Pappy's, my favorite tavern (its clientele being comprised of more locals than golfers), in good cheer.

"Jeez, Lainey. What's up with you? You meet someone last night after I left?" Jessica, my best friend and bartender, grinned at me and poured me a draft.

"No, I'm not that lucky. It just wasn't as crappy a day as usual. What's going on here?"

"As crappy a day as usual," she said.

"When you get off, you wanna hang out for a while?"

"Sure, for a little while. At least until the bad boys file in and creep up the joint. I've got laundry to do anyway."

Jessica moved down the bar to pick up the empty glasses left by a departing tourist couple. She called to them pleasantly, "See you folks. Have a nice trip."

I swiveled around to see if there was anyone fun I could sit with until Jessica's replacement came in. Two bikers were shooting pool, their girlfriends yakking it up at a booth, and only one other guy at the end of the bar. Twitch, a sweet little geezer of about ninety-nine, waggled one finger on his hand holding the beer glass.

"Hey there, Lainey. Whaddaya say?"

"Hey, Twitch. Not much. How you doin'?"

"Still breathing," he said as he took a sip from his ever-present half glass of beer. That was the thing I could never figure out. How come every time I saw him, his glass seemed to have the same amount in it?

"Way to go." I moved down and took the barstool next to him. "Let me ask you something, Twitch."

"Shoot."

"How long have you been in Eden Beach?"

"Oh, let's see. My wife and I moved here shortly after the war, from eastern Oregon. Farming wasn't too good for us there. So, hmm, I guess it's been over sixty years."

"Did you work anywhere besides the mill in all that time?"

"Nope. Didn't need to."

"Wow. I can't even imagine what it would be like to work in the same place like that, day after day, for that long, like forever."

I quickly looked away and took a drink of my beer, afraid that I might have insulted him. But the thought of being so satisfied with a job that you stayed with it for decades fizzled my good mood like salt on a nickel head of foam.

"Ahh, you're still young. Things'll fall into place," he said, getting right to the basic problem.

"I don't know. This town just gets me down sometimes. Nothing going for it besides tourists and golf."

"Just about. At lease since the mill shut down and the fishing industry went belly up."

"Yeah, that was another one of my career-choice failures."

"Not your fault, Lainey. That guy you fished with…" Twitch *tsk-tsked* and shook his head.

Jessica joined us across the bar. "You guys need to be topped off before my shift ends?"

When things were slow, Jessica had a knack for sneaking a refill from the tap for her special friends, like me and Twitch. I nudged my glass over to her and noticed for the first time since I'd sat down that the level in Twitch's glass had changed. It was drained – nothing but foam.

"No, thanks, Jess. Gotta go," he said, and shuffled his tiny self out the door.

"See ya, Twitch. And, hey, thanks for the pep talk."

Jessica brought my full glass back and set it in front of me. "What now? 'Screaming' Bluffs getting to you?"

"Sort of."

"Shit, Lainey. At least you get to see some good-looking golfers. All I get in here are the loopers, and they're so self-medicated by then that I'd probably have more luck taking Twitch home. The rich golfers think they're too good for this dive. The only time they come into town is when they're slumming for sluts, and then they go to the Garden."

The Garden of Eden Lounge was the hard liquor bar at the other end of the block. Taverns serve beer, lounges serve booze and food. At the Garden, *food* was a broad term. To Jessica, all the single women in town, besides us, were sluts.

"Golfers aren't all that good-looking. Besides, they're all married."

"So? When has that stopped you?"

"Shut up. It stops me."

Jessica snorted. "What about Rick the Prick?"

7

"You know that was an accident. He told me his wife left him."

"Yeah. She left him for all of two weeks to go visit her mother."

I sighed. "He made it sound good, the prick."

"Yeah, and the fact that he had a hunky bod didn't hurt." She sighed too. "Oh well, it was good while it lasted, huh?"

We laughed at the memory and Jessica went to close out the till. Curly, the night bartender, was hanging up his coat and taking a look around.

"Not much doin' in here, is there?"

As if on cue, the door swung open, letting in a blast of wind and loud caddies.

"Hey, Tits-well!" Rocks, the scourgiest of the scourge, never got tired of his own jokes. "What kinda tip did ya make today? Sure hope you didn't get turf stains on your knees when you..."

"Whoa, whoa, whoa." Curly, all 300 pounds of him, was quick to my defense. "You're disgusting, Rocks. Leave that foul mouth at the door or I may have to start my shift with an ass-kicking. Wait a minute. That isn't a bad thing, is it?"

Jessica answered smoothly, "Not at all."

I swiveled my stool to look at the group. These were the double-baggers, the hard-asses who tried every day to do a "dub-dub" – carrying two bags for two loops. By their postures, I could tell that their ill-gotten pain meds hadn't compensated for the brutal wind, eighty pounds of clubs, and the fast pace that they subjected themselves to.

"Easy, easy, big boy," Rocks backpedaled. "We'll play nice, okay?" He smiled his crooked, toothy grin at me, a look Jessica says gets all the bar babes drooling after him. It always makes me think of the "special-needs" kid who mainstreamed in my 3rd grade class, except that kid had *way* more going for him.

Jessica wove her way through the group with elbows out and her pint of beer protected. "Beat it, bozos. That's my barstool."

Rocks and his crew slid away and went about their routine. Tick, the small dude in the navy watch cap, sat down by himself with a Guinness, staring straight ahead. Corky, dressed in his usual off-course uniform (a sweatshirt with a mock logo of the "Survivor" TV show that read "I Survived Singing Bluffs" and a white cap with "Looper" printed on it) followed his hero, Rocks, to the video poker game. Hands took his beer and his cell phone over to the window where the reception was better. And Spider, the tall, scary one, took his beer halfway down the bar, but didn't sit. He paced between the TV at the far end, which was showing what looked like an old Bruce Lee movie, and the TV at the other end of the bar with a cooking show.

There were two other guys I didn't know, each sporting the unmistakable mark of a caddie (red-faced from the hat brim down except for the white eye rings left by sunglasses). They sat by the Bruce Lee movie and carried on a loud conversation using "mother-fucker" in more word forms than I thought possible.

I nudged Jessica. "Drink up. Let's get out of here. Did you walk? Need a ride?"

"Nah," Jessica said. "My heap's out back, loaded with my laundry. You doing anything later? Wanna come over to watch something? I've got leftover chicken."

"I don't think so. I'm done for today. And Larson might get me on an early bag tomorrow if I don't look as hungover as these dickheads."

CHAPTER 2

I LIVE IN a shingled two-room house off the main drag. It suits us just fine, since my pooch Rover and I don't need much room. He's a black, shaggy terrier-mix and, like me, he's small with a big attitude. Most of the time he goes with me and waits in the Jeep with the windows down. He can jump out and climb back in whenever he wants, so he's happy. When I do leave him home, he hangs out in his doghouse or cruises his turf. Our residential neighborhood has mostly unpaved roads and a couple of empty lots where Rover goes to do his business, and everyone is used to seeing him strut his stuff around like he owns the place. All the town cops know him and know that he's street-wise, so they leave him alone. By now they know they can't catch him anyway.

Rover was lying on the front porch when I pulled up. His tail wagged and his floppy ears perked up, but that was the extent of the greeting. We have a casually independent relationship.

"Hey, pal, how ya' doin'? Don't get up – I didn't bring you anything."

I stepped through the front door, leaving it open so Rover could take his time deciding whether or not to come in. The door is the only part of the house's exterior that is painted. Shiny, enameled hot pink. I think it's the same shade Superstar Barbie wore. Whenever I tell anyone where I live, they say, "Oh, the house with the hot pink door," like that confirmed just what they'd been thinking about me. I detest the color, but the landlord says it stays until it wears off. I'm pretty sure the door will be standing long after the rest of the POS self-destructs.

It was starting to get dark and cold outside, so Rover moved inside and curled up on his rug next to the wall heater. The couple of beers I'd had at Pappy's had held off my hunger temporarily, but by now the hotdog I'd grabbed at the caddie shack was a distant memory. I was wishing I had taken Jessica up on her invitation to leftovers. I looked in the rust-stained Frigidaire before remembering that, once again, I'd neglected to go to the grocery store. Green spots on the cheese showed through the plastic wrap, and the bread bag had nothing to offer but the same two heels I'd been pushing around for days. I sliced the parts of the cheese that were still orange into Rover's bowl, added some kibble and set it on the floor. He pranced to it energetically and began munching away.

"You're so lucky to have an iron stomach and low flavor standards."

I promised myself to get up early enough for breakfast at the Garden, and I headed to bed.

IF SOMEONE IN Eden Beach says they work "out at the Bluffs" (that's about half the town) they're talking about Singing Bluffs Resort. Except some locals call the place 'Screaming' Bluffs because of the ripping winds. The first course, "The Bluffs," opened four years ago, followed two years later by "Hemlock Hollows," known simply as "The Hollows." There are two driving ranges, a chipping area, and three practice greens. The resort has a fine-dining restaurant, a lounge, a pub, and guest lodging. Each course has its own distinctive design, but the terrains are similar and all of it is built on sedimentary rock and sandy soils forested with evergreens. The course designers left a few trees standing, and some brushy areas of wild plants like Scotch broom, huckleberry and rhododendron.

For me, the best part of caddying here is the environment. I love the blend of natural elements, the meandering walk from forest to meadow to dunes with panoramic views of the Pacific. The unique thing about Singing Bluffs is how the layout works with Mother Nature, using the wind-sculpted hummocks and hollows that provide their own strategic challenges for each hole. The fairways aren't the level, green strips of manicured lawn that I was used to seeing on TV. Instead, there are spots of grass where your tee shot should land and lots of rough everywhere else. The courses look like wilderness landscapes that just happen to include golf holes.

Most of the time, the caddie's main job is to keep the ball in sight, which is challenging in the 80-mile-per-hour wind gusts and moisture-laden skies of summertime in the Pacific Northwest (not to mention the less than stellar abilities of some golfers). That's why one of the best investments for a novice caddie is a good pair of Oakleys. You can get by with decent $50 sneakers, but you'd better put some good money into your shades. Mine have jet-black frames with amber and grey Polarized lenses, and I look stunning in them. I manage to tuck most of my dark, unruly curls into my cap in such a way that keeps the hat on and the wisps from blowing in my face, and when I wear lip gloss and silver hoop earrings I don't look half bad. Not that I want to get my tips based on that, but I don't want to look like just another guy either. And because we all have to wear the same white uniform jumpsuit, it isn't easy.

When I walked into the caddie shack that morning, my bud Tucson Johnny greeted me with a wink and a gleaming smile.

"Hey there, gorgeous." He looked me up and down. "You know, Lainey, I got a lotta respect for you."

"Me? What'd I do?"

"You're not only good-lookin', you're smart. You're not one of these girl caddies that just pops the 150 button, thinking that's all she's gotta do."

"Pops the 150 button? What the hell is that?"

"That's what I call it. When a chick unbuttons her whites to show a lot of cleavage, she's going for the $150 round – the fee plus a $100 tip. You never do that, Lainey. And with your rack, that's really showing some class."

Tucson Johnny is one of the nomadic caddies who works here in the high season, then follows the sun to Arizona or So-Cal for the winter. He's a little rough around the edges, but a real sweetie who's given me lots of pointers about the game.

"Yeah, well, I may not be making $100 tips like some girls, but I think I'll outlast them."

"That's for damn sure, kid. Damn sure."

Of the other women caddies, I knew which ones Tucson Johnny was talking about. One was named Starla... Twila... something like that, and her perpetually runny nose and jitters were a strong indication of fondness for cocaine. She hadn't spoken a word to me since she started, two or three weeks into the season, which I initially thought was weird because of how friendly Tiny Sue was.

Tiny Sue was here in May at the very beginning of the high season. I had just come back from my flop with the commercial fishing gig, and then I took the caddie training class. The ultimate test for a new caddie is to carry the bag a full loop for a senior caddie, and the senior scores your abilities for the manager. This was Tiny Sue's third season at Singing Bluffs, and I was lucky enough to get assigned to her for my test. At five-two, she's slightly taller than me and toothpick thin, always with a perfect manicure. She gave me a decent score, and showed me how to sew a fold in the waist of my whites so the crotch wouldn't hang to my knees. We must have looked like two white leprechauns out on the course. Occasionally the morons in the shack try to goad us into a fight to make their playground dreams come true, but she is way too cool for that. Tiny Sue would never stoop to popping the 150 button.

The other girl I've only seen once or twice in the staging area, but I've heard the guys talk. By the way she was posturing like a streetwalker, there might be something to what they said. I did notice that all eyes were on her as I passed by. It gave me a creepy feeling that made me hunch over and take off my earrings. Some girls you just don't want to be identified with.

Larson called out to Tucson Johnny, "The guest is Hanson, and he's teeing off at the Bluffs in twenty."

"Yes, sir." He bounced up, buttoned up his whites and headed for the staging area.

"Hey Johnny, do me a favor?" I called to him.

"Sure, Lainey. What do you need?"

"I brought Rover today. If you get back before I do, could you..."

"Say no more, sweet lady. I'll make sure he's not harassing the seagulls or taking dumps on the greens."

Larson's head snapped in my direction. "Tidwell, if that dog gets near the playing area..."

"Don't worry, Mr. Larson. Rover stays right by the car, and if he sees anyone coming, he climbs back in the window."

"It's true, boss. I've seen him do it." Tucson Johnny nodded enthusiastically. "He jumps on the running board and scampers into that Jeep like nobody's business. Then he looks back at you like, 'What?' It's the funniest damn thing."

Larson swung his clipboard at him in a fake backhand. "Get out of here."

"I'm gone. Don't worry, Lainey, I'll check on Rover."

"Thanks, Johnny."

Tucson Johnny was lucky to have gotten out early. At nine-thirty a few of us were still waiting for assignments, two of them seniors. At ten I saw Rocks and Corky put out their smokes at the door and come in.

"Morning all. Another beautiful day in Paradise, isn't it?"

16

Two young guys who were playing cards at the back table greeted Rocks, but the two senior caddies looked up from their paperbacks to give him the evil eye. That's the problem with the free-agent rotation system. When it's slow, the seniors can take days off without repercussions, but if they want to work anyway, they are no better off than losers like Rocks and Corky who could waltz in at ten and pick up a bag. Some of these guys had been ready to work since I got here at six-thirty, but the resort wasn't busy enough yet to place them.

I hope they noticed that I was here early. I hope they don't ever give me the evil eye.

Within the next ten minutes Larson got calls for two foursomes, one at each course, that sent six of us out. Thankfully, I was not in the same group as Rocks. The senior who'd been assigned with my foursome hustled out to the Hollows staging area ahead of me and another first-year.

When we caught up to him, he put out his hand for a shake.

"You're Lainey? I'm Jake."

"Hi, Jake." I shook his hand awkwardly, not used to the courtesy.

The other first-year caddie bounded in like a puppy with a new trick. "I'm Pete. They call me Jug Ears."

Poor guy. He really did have quite a pair of cab doors on him. I liked Jug Ears though. He was fun around the shack, always cracking jokes. And not gross ones like Rocks and his boys.

Jake, on the other hand, was the ruggedly handsome silent type. I sometimes can't take my eyes off him, but I know he's married so I try to be discreet. I'd never been this close before, so I hope to god I don't make a fool out of myself today.

The guest services shuttle pulled up with our four players, two of them who greeted Jake with handshakes and back slaps.

"Hey, Jake. Glad you were available," one said.

"Good to see you again, Mr. Hirschman. Mr. Fields."

Hirschman gestured to the other two. "Jake, this here is Sid Lang, and the young punk is Grant Garner."

A slender guy with muscular shoulders stood next to a bag, putting on his glove.

Jake took charge, introducing Pete to Sid and me to Grant.

"You're Lainey? You're my caddie?"

I guessed him to be close to thirty, maybe ten years younger than the others. His eyes were a startling green and he had gorgeous little wrinkles in the corners when he smiled. I knew that it was going to be tough keeping my head in the game today.

"Yes, Mr. Garner. Glad to meet you, sir." I dipped my head and moved to pick up his bag.

"Boy, I guess it's a good thing I don't have a tour bag. Are you sure you can handle this for a full 18?"

"No problem, Mr. Garner. I'm stronger than I look."

Jake smiled at me and hefted the second of the two bags he was carrying.

"She can handle it, sir. She's one of the best caddies we've got."

Some days this is the best job in the world.

A burst of energy known as Kelly, our regular starter at the Hollows, emerged from the shed they call the "curtain" with clipboard in hand. She made sure we were all properly introduced, then gave her cheerful recital of the Starter Speech.

"We expect Ready Play of course, gentlemen, and the rangers will be available if you need assistance of any kind. You've got your score cards, yardage books... just let us know if there is anything else we can help you with. The foursome ahead of you is on the green so you're good to go. Have a wonderful day, sirs."

Into her chest-pocketed radio she announced, "Four with three – Jake, Lainey, and Pete – teeing one at Hollows."

And the seven of us trooped off to the No. 1 tee box.

CHAPTER 3

"IS THIS YOUR first time at Singing Bluffs, Mr. Garner?"

"It is. My associates," he threw his chin in the direction of the three players behind us, "told me about this place. Said it's a one-of-a-kind experience."

"It's all that and more. You're not going to believe the layout, the view… it's beautiful." My mouth was running without help from my brain. I kept up with his fast stride, hoping the brain would catch up before I had to speak again.

"You don't have to give me the sales pitch, Lainey. I've already heard it."

Okay. Good. Just walk, Tidwell. You can do this. Keep a lid on it.

At the first tee, Mr. Garner pulled his driver from the bag before I even set it down, and went to the tee-markers. He took only two practice swings away from the teed ball, then stepped up, took a comfortable swing and shot a straight 220-yard drive to the right side of the fairway.

"Nice shot, Mr. Garner. Looks like you've already figured out how to play into the fan out here. That's something first-timers usually underestimate."

"I did my homework. The wind here is a lot like they get in Hawaii, but more – refreshing."

He wrinkled his crazy green eyes at me and I almost dropped his driver as he handed it over. I recovered in time to pick up his tee and step away for the second guy up.

When all four players had teed off (Mr. Garner lying the best for the approach) we took off at a fast clip.

I was silent, still trying to get a feel for this guy, when he said, "How long have you been caddying?"

"About four weeks." That sounded lame, so I added, "Since you're so hot, doing your homework and all, why did you ask for a caddie?" Shit. I can't believe I said that. "I mean, if you don't mind my asking."

I saw his quick smile before I looked down at my feet, just in time to keep from stumbling on the bumpy ground.

"Hirschman told me that would be the best way. Said I could get lost out here without a guide."

"Yeah, that's true. I heard that some players were lost once over on the Bluffs' No. 16. When it got dark they still hadn't shown up. Turns out, the only way they made it back was by following a raccoon family to the garbage bins behind the lodge."

Why do I say these things? Can't I ever keep my mouth shut?

"Followed raccoons?"

"Not really. I just made that up."

"You're kind of a wise-ass, aren't you, Lainey?"

"Yes, sir. Sorry."

"Don't apologize. I think we're going to get along great. What do you say for this approach?"

"You'd do good to stay to the right. It's 186 yards to the front of the green, another 12 to the pin, and there's a nice draw on the right third of the green. If you can put it in the funnel you can beat the wind. It's a one or two club wind coming right at you."

"Excellent."

He hit a four iron, watched his ball land ten yards shy of the green, bounce to the front right and keep rolling towards the pin, an easy two-putt. One of the other players, one of Jake's, yelled, "Whoo-hoo!" and Garner smiled back at him. I took the iron, wiped it down and placed it back in the bag as we walked over to the edge of the fairway to wait for the others.

"You going to play this lucky all day, Grant?" the whoo-hooer asked when he came up to us. His second shot had landed just short of the green, but on the wrong side of the slope. The last two players were on either side of the fairway, fighting the wind and the hillocks.

"This really is beautiful, Fred. Thanks again for dragging me into it."

"I knew you'd love it. Nothing like this place to make you love golf." He gave me a wink and shot out his hand. "Fred Hirschman. How's it going?"

"Fine, Mr. Hirschman. Glad to meet you."

"Don't let Grant here do too much showing off for you today. I want him to lose fair and square, not have any excuses."

"Showing off?" Garner gave us his cute, crinkle-eyed smile. "When do I ever show off at golf? This is a pure, self-challenging, soul-enhancing game. We compete only with ourselves, for the sheer enjoyment of the sport, for the mental stimulation."

"And for a couple hundred dollars a round, if I remember the bet correctly," Hirschman said with another wink in my direction. I was starting to like him.

The others caught up with us and we headed for the green. Jake gave me a look as he passed by, which I took as brotherly concern for my welfare, and I nodded with what I meant as a professional salute. Who knows what it really looked like? Maybe he thought I was burping out loud. Again.

It had turned out to be a nice day, with just enough clouds over the ocean to make a perfect background for the rocky coastline. The wind was blowing a cool ten-to-twenty mph, but no strong gusts yet. With any luck, we'd be in the woods by the time the wind picked up and we wouldn't be affected too much.

The round was going as expected, with Garner scoring one or two over par on the first four holes, matching Hirschman for total score. Fields was just managing to keep up with us, but the fourth guy couldn't swing worth a shit. He held up play while hacking out of the traps or taking a drop, once he'd agreed with Jug Ears that his ball was lost in the rough.

On No. 5 we had turned south and had the wind at our backs. So far, I had given Garner expert advice and kept my wise-ass remarks to a minimum. And that wasn't easy when we got around Mr. Hirschman and Jug Ears because they kept up a running banter of jibes at Jug Ears's player.

"Sid, you seem to be spending a lot of time in the rough today. You sure you've got the balls to play this course?" Hirschman asked as we watched Sid's tee shot shank into the huckleberry bushes.

"Yeah, sure, sure. I'm not losing any more than usual," Sid said with a straight face. Besides being a poor golfer, he had absolutely no sense of humor. The jokes didn't seem to faze him, so at least there was no harm done.

Jug Ears grinned. "Got it covered, Mr. Hirschman. He's got the balls alright, but he is having trouble keeping it long and straight."

Fields spewed a mouthful of beer. "Oh, cheap shot, Pete." As if he'd never heard that one before. "Lighten up on us weekend duffers, will ya?" He staggered abruptly and nearly fell over, but like an experienced drunk, managed to catch himself.

Jake tried to signal Jug Ears with a shake of his head when the three of us caught up with each other behind the players. Jug Ears missed the warning, but it reminded me to keep a firm bite on my tongue. It was great watching Jake as he handled his two bags with ease. His advice on playing the course was keeping Hirschman happy. Fields, on the other hand, was getting a little too happy, slogging back the beers. I wondered how he was going to last the day. I could see why they had asked for Jake. He didn't bat an eye when Fields spilled a can of beer into his golf bag, just quickly wiped down the clubs with his towel as if nothing unusual had happened. From the way Jake hefted the bag, I gathered it held a good supply of brewskies and Jake knew the routine.

Garner looked like he enjoyed the joking but didn't lose focus on his game. Every so often, when we were away from the others, the conversation was easy.

"So what are all these trees here? Are they Doug Fir?"

"Mostly. There's shore pine, hemlock, and a few red cedars and spruce. The undergrowth is salal, huckleberry, some manzanita. The grounds crew manages to keep the blackberries out."

"Man. I've never seen this many trees on a golf course. It's like playing through a freakin' forest."

I smiled at him. "Yeah. Cool, huh?"

We were starting to climb now, pulling up the switchback trail to the tiered green. He'd played it perfectly, taking my advice to land it with his 6-iron to cross the gully and put it on the same tier as the hole. I loved it when I was right.

"So how come you know so much about the trees and stuff? Did you grow up here?"

"No, I came here from Nor-Cal a couple years ago."

"Nor-Cal?"

"Yeah. That's what we have to say to make sure the natives don't mistake us for Disneylanders."

He surprised me with a laugh. "I don't think you could ever be mistaken for a Disneylander."

"Oh yeah? Why not?" I wasn't sure whether he'd meant it as a compliment or a putdown.

"Lainey, from what I can tell, you are as authentic as they come, and Oregon should be damn glad to have you."

Whew.

"What part of Northern California did you come from?"

"Around Eureka. It was a great place to grow up, but then it got sort of crowded for me. I like small towns."

We'd gotten to the green and looked back to see that we had another wait before anyone else got this far. Garner took a seat on the back side of the green in the shade. I set his bag down and joined him. The familiarity of the environment gave me reassurance. I couldn't remember ever having sat there with a guest before.

We watched Hirschman's ball land in a sand trap below the green, and then Fields and Sid followed, aiming their shots shorter and better placed for their approaches.

Garner picked a blade of high grass off the fringe and began chewing it as he gazed at the ocean on the horizon. "Small towns. I'd like to think I could be myself anywhere, but small-town life scares the shit out of me."

"You kidding me? What the hell is there to be afraid of? It's not like some high school dropout is going to roll you. They don't have that much ambition here."

He laughed. I was impressed with myself that I could make a hotshot guy like him laugh and I wasn't even trying.

"Lainey, you have no idea how lucky you are."

I turned to look at him, waiting for more to that sentence, but by then all three approach shots had bounced on to the green. Garner spit out the grass blade, stood and twisted his torso right and left in an easy stretch, and went to meet the others. I was still sitting there looking stupid when Jake stepped out of the trees onto the fringe. He glanced in my direction without saying anything and put his bags down. Hirschman and Jug Ears were right behind him. I snapped to and went to pull the flag as Fields and Sid came puffing up the hill.

"You two have a nice picnic while we were suffering down there?" Hirschman smiled, but no winks this time.

Garner grinned. "Didn't do too well on this one, buddy?"

"I should've listened to Jake. He told me to lay up but I thought I could make it with my 5-iron. I'm lying par and I'll be lucky to can it in two."

"You've got to watch the undulations here," Jake said to Hirschman and Fields.

Jug Ears handed Sid a putter and said, "We call this green Rock Hudson. It rolls both ways."

Fields cracked up, Hirschman and Garner shook their heads, and Jake busied himself with putters. Sid looked as if he was thinking it over as he studied the green. His ball was the farthest away, so we waited for him to putt first. He picked a piece of grass and let the wind carry it. Then he got on one knee and plumb-bobbed his putter with an outstretched arm, eying the line from his ball to the hole.

"Oh for Christ sakes, Sid. Just hit the ball," Fields yelled. The other two players laughed.

Sid finally putted, his ball curving left, then right, ending up only ten yards closer and still a lousy lie.

"See what I mean?"

"I think he's got it, Ears," I said. "No need to rub it in. Tough break, sir."

"That's quite all right, Miss," Sid said. He walked briskly to his ball and replaced it with a ball marker. "Pete here is doing fine. He's a good caddie for me. Keeps me on my toes."

"Yeah, great, Sid. Now move outta the way and shut up. I'm trying to play here." Fields swayed unevenly as he took a stance at his ball. Without any preamble, he gave it a hard tap that sent it straight over the bumps and valleys, stopping three feet short of the hole. I'll never figure out how drunks do that.

"Nice shot, Mr. Fields," said Jake.

"Jesus, Eddie. You're going to make par." Hirschman was none too cheery as he walked to his ball. His putting was pretty good, so I thought maybe he'd get his two-putt and be Happy Hirschman again. He hit it good and solid and it rolled straight at the hole, but skirted the lip and rolled into a dip.

We all groaned in sympathy. Jug Ears began, "We call that a..."

Jake cut him off. "Don't say it, Pete."

Jug Ears did as advised and quickly moved to help Fields line up his next shot.

When they finally finished the hole and we were headed to the tee box at No. 6, with no one talking about scores, Garner got close and whispered, "What was Pete going to say about Fred missing that putt. What do you call it?"

"Not me. But the boys..." I rolled my eyes.

"Okay, then. What do the boys call it?"

"If I tell you, you have to tell me what you meant when you said I was lucky."

"It's a deal. What do they call it?"

"It's stupid." I looked back to make sure no one else heard. "It's a prom queen."

He waited.

"Because you get a little lip, but no hole."

Garner chuckled once, then shook his head.

"I told you it was stupid. And please don't tell Mr. Fields or he'll repeat it every chance he gets."

"You're probably right about that. Ah, the things you have to put up with around here. Maybe you're not so lucky after all." He grinned at me, took his driver out of the bag and went ahead to the tee box.

As the day progressed, all players seemed to be having a satisfying round, even considering the brief meltdowns. I got a real education working with Jake, seeing how he smooth-talked his players over the rough spots. On the back nine, Hirschman fluffed his third chip shot in a row and was getting close to tossing clubs.

"Say, Mr. Hirschman, have you tried the Irish stew at the lodge?" Jake walked to Hirschman, deftly took his chipping wedge away from him and began wiping it clean.

"What? Irish stew? No, can't say that I have, Jake." He was still staring at where his shot had ended up, a good twenty yards past the 12th green.

"Well, I highly recommend you try it. The dining room and the pub both have Irish stew on their menus." He handed Hirschman his 9-iron and kept right on walking. "They make it with local lamb. Maybe that's why it's so good. And I think they put some kind of whiskey in it. Don't you think so, Lainey?"

I was standing to the side of the green, waiting with the others. "Don't ask me, Jake. I don't know Irish stew from pork and beans."

"But it's good, right? You've had it?"

"Yeah, it's good."

"That's right. Best I've ever tasted. And that includes my wife's, but don't tell her I said so."

Hirschman looked from Jake to me, back to Jake. Then he took a couple practice swings before stepping up to his ball.

"The Irish stew. With whiskey. Sounds good." He set his stance, took a swing and poked a nice lob onto the green where it rolled straight at the pin.

"It's rippin' cloth now," Jake said cheerfully.

And it did. The ball tapped the flag pin and dropped, giving him a par.

That's how it goes with good caddying. You do whatever it takes to get the golfer in the zone. Sometimes it's relieving the pressure, sometimes it's putting pressure on. I'm not nearly as good as Jake yet, but I'm okay. And getting better.

Of course, it's easier when the golfer plays like Grant Garner.

We finished up a little after three-thirty. Garner won the bet, but Hirschman lost by only two strokes. All four players filled out performance cards at the pro shop, rating our services. They requested the same caddies for eight the next morning, so they must have given us points. Grant shook my hand, leaving three bills in the exchange.

Smiling, he said, "Great job, Lainey. And I look forward to seeing you again tomorrow."

"Thank you, Mr. Garner. It's been a pleasure." I was quite proud of myself. I could even look right into his green eyes without getting woozy.

After he'd walked off with his friends and Jake, Jug Ears and I had headed for the shack, I looked at the bills in my hand before stuffing them into my pocket. It was three fifties. And I hadn't shown a bit of cleavage.

CHAPTER 4

BACK AT THE caddies' parking lot, Rover ran to me with little yips of excitement. Since Larson hadn't said anything but "See you tomorrow" when I left the shack, I assumed my dog had stayed out of trouble.

"Hi ya, boy! What a good dog you are. Let's go somewhere fun, okay?" I opened the Jeep's driver-side door, Rover jumped in and made himself comfortable in the passenger seat. I threw the gym bag containing my whites, towels, extra socks and other just-in-case stuff in the back and we took off. Driving out of the resort's main lot, I saw my foursome next to the dining hall. Garner caught me gawking and gave me a friendly wave that took my breath away.

Darn it! Why do I let myself get all flustered just because he's handsome and charming? I'm going to caddie for him just one more day and then I'll never see him again. So I should be cool. I can do this. I can resist.

"Whaddaya say we go to the beach, pal?" Rover's ears perked up at the "b" word. "I'll take that as a yes. Okay. We're goin' to the beach." His ears did it again, which made me laugh and I rubbed his fuzzy head. This is why I have a dog. He's hardly any trouble and the rewards are definitely worth it. I can always count on him to save me from being crazy.

I drove to a viewpoint on the outskirts of town, and because it was late in the day for tourists and too early for the locals who weren't off work yet, there was only one vehicle there. Rover ran ahead and I climbed down the trail and over the piles of driftwood to sit on a rock closer to the surf. Rover isn't much of a fetch-the-stick-dog, so he was content just to run up and down the beach chasing seagulls and occasionally barking at the waves. It was a little cold but the wind wasn't blowing. The sun hung high in the west where I could see a bank of light grey clouds.

"If I was a fool or a tourist, I'd predict that those clouds aren't enough to bring rain." A woman's voice competed with the gulls and the surf to bring me out of my reverie.

"Hi, Gail. Where'd you come from?" I smiled at the familiar face, a regular beach walker I'd come to know because we both had dogs and our beach schedules were more-or-less the same. The difference was that Gail walked her dog; I sat on a rock and let Rover walk himself.

"Angel and I were over there in the dunes, and Rover found us. He's not much of a watchdog, is he? He let me sneak right up on you."

"I don't know. I think if it were a really big, scary guy with a club and making growling noises, I'm pretty sure Rover would let me know. That's what I'm counting on anyway."

We watched the two dogs romp about, playing keep-away with a stick.

Gail sat on the rock next to me. "God, what a beautiful day, wasn't it? Those clouds will make a nice sunset later, if I remember to look at it."

"I'll probably be in the bar."

Gail laughed. "Yeah, I know. That's where I was when I was your age. Now, I'm in my lounger watching a cop show on TV and looking forward to bed."

"At least you've got someone to go to bed with, handsome son-of-a-gun that he is."

"Looks aren't everything. Stewie snores."

We laughed together easily. Gail's laid-back style was what I loved about her. Probably in her fifties, she reminded me of my mother. Except I don't think my mother did the kind of things that Gail said she'd done in younger days. If Mom did them, thank god she hadn't told me about it.

"That doesn't sound too bad to me. Might even be comforting. Snoring reminds you that you're not alone." I curled my arms around my bent knees in an effort to find warmth. We sat in comfortable silence.

"You know, Lainey, you shouldn't rush things. They have a way of working out, when the time is right. From what I've learned about you, I know you'll end up with your own version of Stewart someday."

Another soulful laugh and she got up, calling Angel back from the stinky dead thing that the two dogs had found irresistible. Angel responded immediately. She was a quick, smart dog and Gail had done a good job training her. A pretty, yellow herding type – Stewart claimed she was 100% Pound Hound. Although Rover was half her size, he loved rough-housing with her and they were the best of friends.

"Glad I ran into you, Lainey," Gail said as we made our way back to our cars.

"Yeah, me too. This was just what I needed."

"You don't get enough fresh air and exercise at the golf course?"

"I get plenty. But it's nice to talk to a woman for a change. I mean a smart one."

"Well, thanks. I'd say the same about you."

"Hey, this is your pick-up? Where's your Mustang?"

"This is Stewie's. We traded for the day so that I can stop at the feed store for hay. Gotta hurry to get there before they close. Bye, Rover. See you two next time. Hang in there, kiddo."

Rover and I got in the Jeep, and when I started it up I looked at the clock on the dash. It was ten to five. Happy Hour at Pappy's.

Since it was Thursday and had been a fairly slow day at Screaming Bluffs, no other caddies were at the bar. Those who had worked finished early and either went home to their loving spouses or had immediately taken off for the casino. Thirty miles north of Eden Beach, there was a casino owned by a local tribe where the unattached caddies loved to take their cash. I couldn't understand it, but evidently it was nothing to them to go there and drop their week's earnings, running into the $1000s if they double-bagged twice a day. Occasionally, tales in the shack the next morning were told repeatedly of the killing so-and-so made at the blackjack table, or whatever their game of choice was. If it were someone halfway nice, like Tick or Jug Ears, I was happy for them, but sad to consider how much they'd lost before and that this was all they had to spend their money on. It reminded me of the fishermen I'd worked with recently who spent their hard-earned money on... on what? I don't even know. I didn't stick around that long. But I know it wasn't anything close to a stable family life.

Jessica and I had a fun evening with the locals at Pappy's, playing pool for beers and having some laughs. As a test of strength, I resisted telling her about Grant Garner. Just goes to show you how mature I can be.

PROMPTLY AT 7:30 the next morning I checked in with Larson at the caddie shack, then caught up with Jake and Jug Ears as the shuttle pulled to a stop. Our guests were playing the Bluffs today, which was a half-mile jaunt from the caddie shack to the other side of the resort. Because I had advance notice, I'd left Rover at home in charge of the neighborhood for the day. He liked variety, and I'm almost positive that he sees more action there than in the caddie shack parking lot.

Jake said, "Morning, Lainey."

The shuttle driver said "Good morning, little lady." He was one of the old guys who drives caddies as well as guests around the resort, or into town when there's nothing else to do.

"Hi, guys. Let's roll," I said as I took a seat, continuing with the last-minute job of tucking my hair in my hat. From the lack of chatter on the ride, I guessed that Jake had given Jug Ears a heads-up regarding his joking around so much the day before. Ears gave me a polite smile and then seemed to think that his golf towels needed immediate attention.

"Yo, Jug Ears. How's it going?"

He kept refolding and stuffing towels into the pockets of his whites, as if too absorbed in the chore to answer.

Our players joined us at the Bluffs staging area. Garner looked sharp in forest green, lightweight cords, and a white polo shirt minus the ubiquitous sports logo. I loved that he didn't wear a cap to spoil the look of his wind-blown, dark blond hair. He was a hunk, but not so proud of his muscular arms to go jacketless all day; I saw an expensive Gore-Tex jacket in his bag. Mr. Hirschman was decked out in Singing Bluffs trousers, shirt, vest, windbreaker and snap-brim hat – the full advertising package. Fields looked like he'd pulled his khakis and sweatshirt out of a gym bag, and he had done a lousy job of shaving. His bloodshot eyes were probably a clue to the reason for that. And good old Sid's polyester outfit was so brightly colored he looked like a parrot.

After the circuit of greetings was completed, I decided I could venture a jab at Hirschman.

"I see you did a little shopping in the pro shop, Mr. Hirschman. Lookin' pretty snazzy." I winked at him, which provoked a nervous look from Jug Ears, but Jake laughed with the others.

"No kidding he did a little shopping," Garner said. "Fred always brings an extra suitcase to haul back all the crap he buys at golf resorts."

"Now, now. Don't you be poking fun, just because I happen to like supporting the economy of friendly little clubs like this. A few souvenirs with the club's logo shows that I enjoyed my stay."

Fields joined in. "And shows your wife that you actually went golfing and not to some sunny beach with your secretary."

"See what you've started, Lainey." Hirschman said. "I guess the only way to combat this ridicule and regain my pride is to beat the tar out of these boys in a round of golf." He picked up his own bag and marched ahead, with Jake striding easily behind him. A few feet away Hirschman let Jake take the bag. Jake pulled it over his left shoulder, adjusting the weight of Fields's bag on his right without breaking his pace. Ears and I picked up our bags and followed in Jake's footsteps.

"We took Jake's advice and ate in the lodge last night, Lainey," Garner said as we walked together to the first tee box. "But I'm going to be bored with this place by the end of today. I was hoping you'd tell me about a good place in town."

"You're not going to find the fine dining like you're used to in Seattle. I'll tell you that, Mr. Garner."

He stopped walking and gave me a stern look. "First of all, I'm not the snob you think I am. I even eat grilled cheese sandwiches and canned tomato soup sometimes. And second of all, call me Grant, not Mr. Garner. It makes me feel like I'm at work and I'm having too much fun to even think of work. And third of all..."

"Grant, quit your yakking and tee up," Hirschman called to him. "Let's see who's going to be the Big Kahuna today."

All four started with great drives, and their good moods were accented by the warm, sunny morning. We caddies kept our players happy with clever tips, appropriate compliments, and even though Jug Ears kept his jokes to a minimum, our snappy repartee.

38

When we reached the turn stand, Sid and Hirschman hit the port-a-potties and Fields started for the snack bar.

"I could use a beer. You want one, Grant? I'm buyin'."

"Jesus, Fields. It's ten in the morning. How the hell do you drink so much and stay standing?" Garner asked.

"Practice." Fields took determined strides towards the large shed that housed the snack bar. Inside, one of the local retirees who found seasonal work at the Bluffs more fun than staying home, sold Power Bars, soft drinks, beer, and liquor in those little airliner bottles.

"I'm going to get a Pepsi. Can I get you something, Lainey?" Garner asked.

"A Diet Pepsi would be great, thanks." To be safe, I left off both the "Mr. Garner" and the "Grant."

Jake approached me with a quizzical expression. "How's it going, Lainey?"

"I'm doing great. How about you?"

"Okay. Just checking."

He turned away and I said, "Hey, Jake, it's nice how you look after us first-years. I think Ears would be sounding like Rodney Dangerfield if you hadn't cooled his jets."

"Yeah, well. He's a good dude. Don't want to see him get bounced." With that, Jake walked off.

Garner came out of the tent, opened a can of pop and handed it to me.

"Thank you."

"Sure. What's up for this next hole, caddie?" He was having fun, looking like a kid swinging his driver with one hand, taking drinks of his soda with the other.

"You'll want to drive hard up the middle, then lay up on the approach. Keep it low to stay out of the crosswind."

"Ha! Excellent." He called back to the others, "Let's go, kiddies. I have my plan of attack!" and hustled off before he could hear any of their replies.

I was right on his heels. After everyone teed off, we followed his perfectly hit ball down the fairway. When we were out of earshot from the other players, I asked, "So what's third of all?"

"What?" He crinkled his eyes at me.

"You were giving me the list. You sometimes eat grilled cheese sandwiches, and you don't want to be called Mr. Garner. What's the third thing?"

He stopped walking and faced me. "You, Lainey. You're the third thing."

Now it was my turn to say, "What?"

"You give the impression that you think of yourself as some small-town hick with a dead-end job. Well, lighten up. You're a lot more together than you give yourself credit for. You're smart, cute as hell, funny, and talented." He spread his arms wide, taking in the landscape. "And this is no dead-end job, believe me. So quit putting yourself down and enjoy your beautiful life."

I hadn't really heard anything past "cute as hell."

CHAPTER 5

WHEN I PARKED my Jeep in the driveway, Rover bounded out of his doghouse with more enthusiasm than usual.

"What have you been up to, mister? If you weren't fixed I'd think you'd been fooling around with your neighborhood girlfriends. Maybe just wishing you could, huh, buddy?" I squatted to scratch his ears and let him lick my face. "What a sweet doggie you are. What a good boy." I dropped my gym bag and picked Rover up to give him a proper hug. We had a sloppy moment of kissing and hugging, the show of affection that only dog owners know.

Once inside and settled on the crummy couch with a box of Cheez-its tucked under my arm, I cracked open a bottle of beer and put my feet on the coffee table. It was actually an overturned fish box that I'd found on the beach, made of rough planks that had dried to a shiny grey and had only a whiff of beachy smell. It suited the purpose, and the price was right.

Rover jumped up next to me, understandably more interested in the crackers than in me. I gave him one, took a handful for myself, and had a pull on my beer. Then fear set in. I was about to go out on a date. I hadn't had a date since high school, and I hated them then. Something about getting dressed up and prepared like a Thanksgiving turkey with all the trimmings, to be the exclusive property of one guy for a whole evening, turned my stomach.

"Oh jeez, Rover, what have I done now?" Rover only sniffed at my hand and I gave him one of my crackers.

It had been a casual, spur-of-the-moment answer to Grant's invitation to show him Eden Beach. He said, "Show me what the town looks like, then we'll grab some dinner." No big deal. Caddies probably did it all the time. Especially the girl caddies.

That was the big deal. A female caddie agreeing to go anywhere with her player was the first step in transacting the deal, the solicitation and procurement of the kind of favors sleazy men expected if they could afford them. And sleazy girls were eager to provide because they were stupid enough to believe it would give them a taste of the glamorous life they'd seen in movies. I hadn't been working at the Bluffs a week before I knew which girls were providing more than the usual services for the guests. From sous chefs to desk clerks, stupid women were flopping on their backsides hoping for their ticket to Paradise.

Did Grant think I was one of those? Was he one of those? He could be married, for all I knew.

"Shit, shit, shit," I told Rover. He wagged, perked up his floppy black ears and drooled with his tongue hanging out the side of his mouth. "Well, it's too late to back out now. I can't lie worth a damn and if I try, I'll look like a bigger fool than I do already. If that's possible."

Rover had no reply.

"You're a big help." I stuffed the remaining handful of Cheez-its in my mouth. After washing it down with several gulps of beer, another problem occurred to me. "Oh shit! What am I going to wear?"

One-and-a-half beers later I was cleaned up, dressed, coifed, and painted. I was ready at 6:45, a full fifteen minutes before for Grant's stated zero hour. I'd rummaged through my clean clothes and finally came up with black cords with flared legs that looked good with my dressy bitch-boots. For just the right dash of color, I wore my fairly new (and therefore unstained) not-too-tight burgundy T-shirt, and put my black Levi jacket over that to try to hide more of my boobs. To look fancy I added a silver necklace and matching droopy earrings.

Studying the mirror, I decided I'd done a decent job of putting myself together – not too dressy, as if I were tarting it up for a meat-market bar crowd, not so casual that I looked like just another caddie coming right off the course. My living room/kitchen was fairly presentable, too, (once I hid the empty beer bottles and snacks) in case I decided to invite him in for a minute.

Now I had nothing to do for fifteen minutes but sit and worry. What if any of the other caddies sees me? Like Rocks! What if he sees me? If he discovered that I went out with a guest, the amount of crap he'd throw at me would be outrageous. I've got to take Grant somewhere where neither Rocks nor any of his spies would hang out. So Pappy's is out – that's a no-brainer. They might be at the Garden, too, especially later if there's a band. We could go to the Chinese restaurant, nobody goes there.

"Rover, what the hell am I going to do?"

Rover jumped up from his napping place at my feet and darted to the door.

"Good idea. Let's go for a walk."

We were stepping off the porch when a white SUV turned into the street. It was Grant, who grinned at us as he parked and got out. His outfit – jeans, a blue and black striped dress shirt cinched alluringly with a soft leather belt that matched his sneakers, and navy fleece jacket – was as equally non-dressy/non-casual as mine.

"Not trying to escape, are you?"

"Oh, no. Hi. Rover and I were just going to get a quick walk. You're early."

"Just a little. So this is Rover." He knelt and Rover immediately jumped all over him, licking Grant's grinning face, nearly pushing him over.

"Get down! Oh jeez, he's getting paw prints all over you."

Grant stood up, brushing himself off with a laugh. "Forget it, it's nothing. Hey, Rover. How ya doin', buddy."

Rover ran in little circles, doing his disgustingly cute routine. He has no shame.

Grant laughed like a ten-year-old.

"Don't encourage him. He shouldn't get away with jumping up on you like that."

"Hey, no problem. He wants a walk, let's walk. You can show me your neighborhood."

Grant cast glances up and down the gravel road, but his eyes kept returning to my hot pink door.

To divert him, I pointed down the street. "You can pretty well see the whole neighborhood from here. Not much to it."

"That's some door." He was still staring. "When you gave me directions you should've told me about the door. I could've seen it from the highway."

"Not my color choice. It was the previous tenant's."

"She must have been interesting."

"Yeah, he was. Or so the neighbors tell me."

"Oh." Then he noticed Rover was nudging his hand. "Well, how about that walk? Let's go to the beach. I've seen it from the golf course so I know you have one."

The beach. Perfect. No caddies will see us there.

"You mean take Rover? Are you sure you want him in your car? He'll be covered with sand on the way back."

"I don't care. Besides, it's a rental. You're not hungry yet, are you? We could go eat first."

"No, I'm fine. The beach is good." I was already getting into the rental, and Rover hopped over me to sit on the armrest.

Grant drove like a tourist through Old Town, while I pointed out the odd little shops that were my favorites. He was appropriately awed.

"So this is Eden Beach. I love the diversity of architectural styles. There isn't that pseudo quaint uniformity that most coastal towns try."

"No. I think merchants here go more for Early Slapdash."

He laughed and I started to relax. I didn't even notice if there were any cars I recognized parked at Pappy's.

"There's the candy store that gives free samples. And across the street is my favorite bakery. I love their sourdough baguettes. Sometimes I go to that fish market over there for crab cocktails, when I can afford it. They've got the best deals and the freshest catch. I try to get whatever's in season."

"Are you sure you're not hungry? We could skip the beach and go straight to dinner."

I laughed. "No, really I'm fine. Turn left at the stop sign, and we'll head for the jetty."

The beach was deserted except for a family packing up their blankets and toys, and a lone walker-with-dog too far away to identify.

"Wow, this is beautiful. You don't get this on Puget Sound." Grant put his face to the onshore breeze and inhaled deeply. "Oregon's got the best beaches."

We walked at the surf line, dodging waves while Rover scampered through the driftwood.

"I like that our coast has more rocks than the beaches up north. The seastacks make huge wave crashes, lots of noise and excitement. You should be here in the winter. It's amazing."

"I should."

The tenderness in his voice made me stop in my tracks just as a sneaker wave hit a nearby rock with a spectacular explosion. Grant cheered, then grabbed my arm and pulled me out of the way before we got wet. I heard a woman's laughter along with Grant's, and there was Gail. She was the lone walker and she'd caught up to us without my noticing.

"That was a close one," Gail said. "Forget to keep your eyes on the ocean, Lainey?"

"Hi, Gail. Nah, I was just goofing off," I said lamely. "Grant, this is Gail. And the one who's about to add more paw prints to your jeans is Angel."

"Hi. I see these two have met before."

The dogs were posing in their usual pray-bows, then chased each other in dangerously close circles around us.

"Come on, Angel, this way. It was nice to meet you, Grant. Enjoy your walk." She smiled at me and moved on, Angel finally giving up her game and following.

"Incredible. Running into people you know just doesn't happen in Seattle."

"Happens all the time here. Not always a good thing. But Gail's nice, a good friend to walk with." A friend I know will hold confidences.

"Well, I'm starving. How about you?"

"Yeah, I could eat." I added with emphasis, "There's a good Chinese place up town."

"I'm not crazy about Chinese food. Hope you don't mind, but I made reservations at Rosaria's in case we couldn't decide where to go. The resort people recommend it, and I thought..."

"Hey, that's great! I've never been there." And neither have any other caddies because the prices are out of our pay range. There will be no chance of seeing anyone I know there. "What time are our reservations?"

Grant looked at his watch. "In about ten minutes."

CHAPTER 6

ROSARIA'S DIDN'T LOOK like much from the outside, just a dinky, flat-roofed, shingle-sided building on a side street in Old Town. But as soon as we walked through the door I felt under-dressed. I couldn't remember the last time I'd eaten at a place with white linen table cloths, silver napkin rings, and wine glasses that didn't come from Costco. I think it was... never.

Grant held my chair out for me as the waitress welcomed us. I was still catching my breath when I finally looked up to see that she was my neighbor's kid, Stephanie.

"Hey. Hi."

"Hi, Lainey. I'm so glad to see you here!" And she sounded glad. That was how Stephanie always sounded.

"I didn't know you worked here, Stephanie. How's it going?"

"Great! I love it. You know, it's just for the summer, until courses start at Oregon State."

"Well, good for you." I was doing my darndest to sound casual, and I noticed that Grant was grinning his face off. "Uh, Grant, this is Stephanie. Her folks live on my street. Rover hangs out there a lot. They feed him scraps." Oh, that was intelligent.

"Hi, Stephanie," he said as he rose to take her hand. "Any friend of Rover's is a friend of mine."

She giggled, of course, as she gave him the wine list, handed us each a tiny menu and finally left us alone. It took me another few breaths to realize that there wasn't anything to worry about; my neighbors never crossed paths with anyone from the resort.

Grant smirked. "Is this coincidental or do you know everyone in town?"

I looked around the dining room carefully. "Nope. There isn't another soul here who I recognize. Of course, I'd have to check out the kitchen staff to be sure."

Grant kept his grin and looked at the menu. "What do you like?"

Between the Italian words and the fancy lettering, I couldn't understand anything but the prices. "Oh, I don't know. I only know what I don't like – mushrooms and oysters."

"Okay, no mushrooms, no oysters. Trust me to order for you?"

"Please do." Now I could forget about the prices.

Stephanie appeared as if from thin air. "May I serve you a wine while you decide what you'll be ordering for dinner?"

"I can give you the whole works right now." Grant smiled at her. "For the antipasti, we'll have the crostata salata di fontina

49

and the mizuna salad. And for the entrees, we'll try the gnocchi verdi and the crab ravioli. Is the crab fresh?"

"Yes, it is fresh Dungeness; the boats were in last night. And all of our pastas are handmade daily. I'm sure you'll enjoy your choices. Would you like anything else?"

"I love the Willamette Valley wines. We'll have a bottle of Kings Estate Pinot Gris, please."

Stephanie took our menus, smiled pleasantly, and said, "Very good. I'll bring that right away, sir." She hadn't written anything down.

"Wow." I watched her maneuver through the tightly packed room to the kitchen.

Grant beamed at me. "How'd I do? Pretty good, huh?"

"Oh, yeah, you did okay. But I'm impressed with Stephanie. I didn't know she could focus like that. So, what are we eating?"

"You'll see. I promise it's nothing exotic, just good Italian."

A guy in a white shirt and black vest brought our wine. He poured a small amount for Grant, who sipped and nodded his approval. My glass was poured and I carefully took a swallow, making sure I didn't spill any on my front.

"I forgot to tell you earlier, you look very nice." Grant's smile almost made me swoon.

"Me? You do. You've got a nice dress shirt on and I'm wearing a crummy T-shirt." I looked down at myself for emphasis, realizing too late that my gesture only brought attention to my big boobs. I felt myself getting red-faced.

Grant didn't even look. "Shush. Just take the compliment and drink your wine."

I did, and looked around the room to give my face time to get itself together. There were five other tables filled, either with tourists or unidentified locals. None looked like golfers. They all seemed to be enjoying themselves and not paying any attention to us. I took another swallow of wine and relaxed.

Stephanie came to our table bearing two huge plates with a small amount of food on each one, then hesitated.

"Put them anywhere," Grant said. "We're sharing."

The food turned out to be a mixed green salad and a cheese tart, not the dessert kind, and they were both fabulous. We forked helpings from each other's plates, and I ate more than my share of both. There was also an endless supply of crusty bread, and a little dish of herbed olive oil for dipping, that I couldn't stop eating.

Between bites I managed to hold up my end of the conversation. We talked comfortably about small-town life, me giving the answers to his questions.

Finally I said, "I've been to Seattle. They have neighbor-hoods. It's not so different from small towns."

"Maybe, but I don't get out to the neighborhoods." Grant leaned back in his chair as our plates were cleared. He drank some wine, set his glass down and eyed it while he turned it in place.

"Why not?"

"I work in the city, eat in the city, sleep in the city. Everything I do is downtown. I don't get out of the high-rise district."

A wistful mood had started to take hold when Stephanie and the guy in the vest brought in our main course plates. More wine was poured and we got busy tasting and passing pasta back and forth. I was sure it was more than I could eat, but I was giving it one hell of a try.

Grant ate with the same gusto he had when he swung a golf club.

"Man, this is good. I can say without a doubt that this is the best Italian dinner I've ever had."

"That's probably really saying something. I'm guessing you eat out a lot." Maybe it was the wine, but I decided to take a stab at getting personal. "So tell me. What is it that you do?"

"I never said?" He shoveled another mouthful.

"No. I figured you were some kind of engineer with Boeing or Microsoft. Isn't everybody in Seattle?"

He was still chewing, so he shook his head while his eyes twinkled a smile.

"No, not everyone." He put down his fork and wiped his mouth with his napkin. "I have my own company. Garner Global Property Management."

"Global? Does that mean you manage properties all over the world?"

"No, just Seattle. But a lot of my clients are foreign investors so I do get to travel some."

"That's why you've golfed in exotic places."

He looked puzzled. "What makes you say that?"

"Yesterday you compared the wind here to the wind on Hawaiian courses." I was so proud of my attention to details. How was it that I hadn't bothered to find out whether he was single?

"Oh, yeah. Well, once in a while, for making business connections." He ate some more ravioli.

"Wow. That's pretty cool. That must be the best part of your job."

"Not even close." He put his fork down and rested his forearms on the table. There was no lack of energy in his mood now. "The best part is downtown Seattle itself... the people who live there. There's an attitude, a good one, about the folks who not only tolerate the wet, salty air, the murky light, the streets crawling with tourists... they thrive on it. And everyone wears a smile, from the drunks at Pioneer Square to the overworked office workers, to the stressed-out fat cats running to their double-parked limos. The sidewalks of downtown are a great equalizer."

At that moment, a robust woman in a white apron came through the swinging doors from the kitchen, smoothing her graying hair with the backs of her hands.

"Hello, hello! How is everyone tonight?" she asked the room, and the room responded with raised glasses, actual applause, and shouts of "Perfetto, Rosaria!" and "Tutto bene!" Grant joined right in. I had no idea there was anything like this in Eden Beach. I applauded politely.

"I'm glad you're enjoying yourselves, your meals. Now I just want to tell you what desserts you can choose from tonight."

A mixture of m-m-m-ms and groans came from the diners.

"Well now. Tonight we have my own tiramisu, made with dark chocolate and my own blueberry preserves, and Spumoni Carlton, which is a caramel ice cream and strawberry ice dish with some glazed strawberries on top. And to be fair, you know Rosaria always tries to be fair to those who cannot indulge as Rosaria wishes, I can whip up a low-calorie

Zabaglione in a flash. So, you contemplate as you finish your meals, and we'll all have a good time, no?"

It was contagious. I was almost giggling as I watched her float back to her kitchen, stopping at a table here and there to say hi to personal friends.

"So where were we?" Grant asked.

"Drunks and fat cats on the sidewalks of downtown Seattle. So which ones do you hang out with, the drunks or the fat cats?"

"Ah, well. I'm sorry to say I don't hang out with anyone. I'd probably be more associated with the smiling, overworked office workers. Me and my staff – there are four of us at the moment."

I pictured the secretary in a well-fitted pencil skirt whose silken hair shaped her face glamorously when he took her glasses off.

"But if you're the boss, why is it you don't get out much?"

"I just love my work. I have more fun showing properties and getting people into a new apartment that they thought they'd never be able to afford. I have a knack for determining whether a possible tenant is a true Seattleite, whether they'll last a winter or bail after the first month of non-stop rain. I'm good at matching people up with their dream home and getting them a deal."

"So no social life? You've got, uh, friends, don't you? Family?"

"Oh, I see Fred Hirschman and one or two other golfing buddies occasionally. And they've tried to fix me up with single girls they know, without success."

He grinned. Fond memories of the chase, or pride in his reputation as unconquerable? I wondered. Anyway, I guess I could stop worrying about his marital status.

"The part I hate about my work, though," Grant continued, "is dealing with the rich bastard developers who come into town with OPM..."

"Wait. What?"

"Other people's money, sorry. They buy up properties, slap on a cheap coat of paint and then raise rents beyond reason."

"Does that happen a lot?"

"Oh, you bet. At least it used to. Maybe it's slowing down now that the market's tanked and the Tenants Union has gathered strength. Anyway, that's what I do. I bully asshole developers to lower rents and I find fellow Seattleites a place to live."

He paused to signal Stephanie, then pointed to the lone bite of gnocchi left on my plate. "Are you going to finish that?"

"No, I don't think so." I was immediately aware of the fold of tummy hanging over the waistband of my pants.

Stephanie bounced to our table, and Grant asked, "Can we get a little box for this? We have a neglected pooch in the car."

"Oh, you sure can. I know Rover will love this." She picked up our plates and I noticed that Rover would score better from Grant's than mine.

"And I'd like some coffee, please."

Stephanie asked, "Caffeinated or not?"

"Caffeinated, please. How about you, Lainey, coffee? Or would you like more wine?"

"No, thank you. Coffee's fine. Caffeinated." What the hell. I wasn't going to be able to fall asleep tonight anyway.

Grant added, "And I'd like to try Rosaria's famous tiramisu. What are you going to have, Lainey?"

"Dessert? Are you kidding? I can't eat another bite."

Thankfully, Stephanie ignored my protest. "Oh, come on, Lainey. Try the Zabaglione. It's to die for."

"Is that the low-cal one?"

"Yes, but you won't even believe it when you taste it."

"I'll have that."

CHAPTER 7

I ACTUALLY SLEPT pretty well, considering my full stomach and my head full of that buzz that happens when I can't stop thinking about a guy. It was a nice, easy buzz though, not the irritating libido-driven clatter that makes me feel like a crazed teenager. I'm positive I fell asleep with a smile on my face, a smile that lasted through my normal Saturday morning routine.

I did have to go to work, and I would probably have to hang out for hours in the shack with a bunch of morons, but I could pass the time pleasantly remembering my date with Grant. After we'd left the restaurant, he drove me home and held my hand as he helped me out of the car and walked me to the door. Then he turned me and planted a perfect, full on two-second kiss right on the mouth. We both giggled. Then he said, "I'll see you again soon, okay? I don't know when, but I sure want to come back."

He had already told me how he had to leave on the first morning flight back to Seattle. Even though it was the weekend, he needed to be at work – something about it being crunch time with rents coming in.

"Well, I'll tell Larson and he can get me assigned as your caddie. That is, if you want."

"No. I mean, if you want to, it's up to you. But I won't really need a caddie, and I was thinking I'd be seeing you, you know, off the course. Can I? If you're not busy?"

"Yeah. I'd like that."

"Okay, good." He let go of my hand to dig for a pencil and a score card he found in his jacket pocket. "Do you have a phone? How can I reach you?"

My cell phone, my only phone, seldom rings and no one ever asks for my number, so I drew a blank. "Uh, wait a minute."

I went in the house, rummaged in pockets of clothes hanging on my bedroom door until I found the phone. While I waited for it to power up, Grant came in and glanced around the living room.

"Nice."

"You're kidding."

"No. I like it. It's you. Small, but has loads of style."

"Thanks." I hurriedly looked down at my phone before he could see me blush. I read out my number and he wrote it on the score card.

"Great. I'll phone you as soon as I can arrange another trip. I had a good time, Lainey, and I can't wait to spend more time with you, to get to know you better." His eyes gave me that gorgeous crinkle. He grinned, then he rushed at me and kissed me again. "Bye, Lainey."

And that was that. It couldn't have been easier.

"WHAT ARE YOU smiling about, Sweetcheeks?"

"Just trying to keep from crying, Rocks. But I get the feeling that's about to change now that you're here."

Rocks leered at me as he took the chair next to mine. His two pals, Hands and Corky, went to check Larson's tee sheets to see how many pre-assigned caddies were scheduled for the week. The fewer senior caddies signed up, the better our chances of getting an early loop. Since it was the middle of the high season, the roster was full. We free-agents had to wait in the bucket.

"Don't you have something better to do?" I tried to block Rocks's stare with the paperback I'd not read a word of since I sat down. Robert B. Parker wasn't holding my attention today.

"No, not really. I think I'll just sit here and try to figure you out."

"What's to figure?"

"I know you got the hots for me, Titswell. You're no different from the other caddie chicks around here. You all try for the boys' club weekenders, but when that doesn't work out you'll give ol' Rocks a turn. I don't have the money that those guys do, but I can give you something that'll make you come back for more."

Talk about a buzz kill.

"Please go away, Rocks. I'm trying really hard not to punch you in the gut right now."

"Ooo – I like to play it rough, too. Why don't we take it to the mat tonight, Sweetcheeks? We could burn it up."

The wind gusted from the side door and Tiny Sue came in. As soon as she caught the look in my eye, she moved to the seat behind Rocks, giving his cap a delicate flick so that it fell over his eyes.

"Quit bothering her, Rocks. When are you going to realize that there's at least a couple of us girls who find you repulsive?"

He took his cap in his hand and made a sweeping bow. "Forgive me, O Great One. I didn't know I was in the presence of Your Royal Highass." With that, he sauntered off to join his buddies.

"What a child," Tiny Sue said.

"He's just jealous. He'd kill to have your rep."

"For fifty bucks and a plane ticket, he can have it."

I'd not seen Tiny Sue in this kind of mood before. She had given me more professional tips than anyone, and I had nothing but the utmost respect for her. But now I sensed that she could use a girlfriend.

"Why are you here, Sue? I mean still here this morning. Aren't you usually one of the first ones out on Saturday?"

"Well, it seems I'm not giving my all, as the pro in management calls it." She let out a huff of breath and sank back into her chair, the cushions enveloping her.

"You're kidding. You're one of the best. The players love you."

"That depends on what you call 'love,' I guess."

"Tell me. What gives?"

"Have you noticed that certain caddies are getting more loops than they deserve, more than other first-years? I'm talking about the other girls."

"I don't know; I hardly ever see them."

"That's because they're out on the courses most of the time. I get here before they do, but as soon as Twila and her pal Cindy walk in, Larson's calling them to the staging areas. It's too weird."

"Yeah, I guess I have seen that happen. It didn't dawn on me. Why were you still waiting? You're a senior. You're on the pre-assigned list."

"Whoever's calling the shots up in management is playing favorites, and I can only guess what those girls are offering in return."

Tick, the little, quiet guy, moved past us and Sue waited. He left out the side door, cigarettes and iPod in hand, without making eye contact.

I wanted to know more. "I've seen those two flirting with guests, and I know what the rumors are. Do you think they're really doing these guys for money?"

"Doing them? Honey, Twila showed me photos of her weekend in Miami, courtesy of one high-roller she caddied for last month."

"You're kidding."

"It wouldn't be the first time an exchange of 'gifts' was arranged out on the fairway. Of course, that's their business, and it doesn't make any difference to me. At least it shouldn't."

"But..."

"I went in to talk to the pro just now, to ask why I was skipped over this morning. He told me that it wouldn't hurt if I was a little friendlier, to the guests and to management. He said he thought I was a little too 'standoffish.'"

"You're shitting me! I can't believe that." I must've gotten a little too loud, because heads turned. No way did I want any of Rocks's snoops to get wind of this. I whispered, "What did you say?"

"I argued, as politely as I could, that none of my players were complaining. And I asked him if he was telling the men caddies to be friendlier. He told me it wasn't about any 'discrimination issues,' that he just wanted to give me some helpful advice." Sue's eyes hardened with a look that would've scared me, if I was a guy. Nice to have her on my side.

"What are you going to do?"

"I don't know, Lainey. I just know that this place sucks."

"Yeah, it does. Sometimes." So much for my joyful memories of last night.

She got up. "Well, I've had enough of this BS today. I'm going home."

"Okay, hang tough. And, Sue? Let's stick together on this. Maybe it will work out. They can't get away with this."

"Sure, Lainey," she laughed. "Life's always fair."

I was left alone again. Well, alone with a room full of guys.

An almost noiseless, immediate commotion swept through the room. I looked around and caught a glimpse of a county sheriff's patrol car pulling up outside. Three caddies who had been in the smoking area flew in the side door and out the back toward the locker rooms. Two guys who had been playing cards in the back corner lifted the window next to them and dove through as if the building were on fire. A couple others picked up their gear and made a nonchalant move for the front door. I looked around to see that only

Tucson Johnny, Jug Ears, and I were left. Larson greeted the deputy and took him into the office.

"Don't worry about it, Lainey," Johnny told me. "It's standard behavior around here. A cop shows up and the culls scatter like squirrels from a hound dog. Usually it's a warrant for an outstanding civil case, or a deadbeat dad beef. Sometimes it's a skip on a court appearance. Sometimes a tip on a drug deal. Whatever. It's funny how many loopers in this place have something to hide, isn't it?"

"HOW WAS LIFE as a blooper today, kid?" Jessica asked as she plopped on the barstool next to me.

"Like I've told you a hundred times, we're called loopers, not bloopers."

"Yeah, that makes sense too. All you caddies seem loopy to me." She took a huge pull on her long-neck Bud, her first since getting out from behind the bar five seconds earlier. "Where were you last night? You missed another Pappy's extreme Friday night – totally crazy as usual and because you weren't here I ended up talking to and almost going home with a trucker, for crisesakes." She took another pull.

I really should've called her from the caddie shack this morning. Jessica is my best friend and I hadn't given her the slightest tidbit about Grant.

"I went out on a date. Well, sort of a date." I winced and tightened my right biceps, preparing for the blow I knew was coming.

She punched me with her right, making sure our beers were well out of range. Even off-duty bartenders hate to see beers spilled.

"You're shittin' me! Who *are* you? A date? Wait. Lainey, you didn't go out with one of those sleaze-ball caddies, did you?"

"What? No. Jess, don't even think it." I took a sip of beer to stall for time. Jessica's glare was singeing the hair on the side of my head.

"It was just a guy I caddied for," I said.

Jessica's eyes popped. "Lainey!" she shrieked, "You hooked a rich golfer! Is he hot? What's he look like? How old?"

"Shut up!" I looked around, but the only people in the bar were tourists and a group of hard-partiers who looked like they'd either gotten an early start on this night's party or forgot to call it quits on last night's. No one was paying any attention to us. "It's no big deal. He's a nice guy from Seattle, just wanted to get off the resort and see some local color, that's all. It wasn't like a real date." I sipped some more. It might've been more of a gulp.

Jessica turned away from me, drinking silently. Finally she said, "This nice guy you caddied for, he wanted to see some local color on a Friday night, and you didn't bring him in here?"

I could see her point. Pappy's was basically the only thing to do in Eden on a Friday night, publicly anyway. And it doesn't get more colorful than Pappy's.

"Have you ever been to Rosaria's, the Italian restaurant down the street?"

"Never heard of it."

"It's a block and a half away. How can you not have heard of it? Jess, you've gotta get out more."

"Oh, ex-cuse me. Who are you, Rachael Ray? All of a sudden beer, free popcorn, and micro-waved burritos aren't good enough for you?"

We waited a good four seconds, then simultaneously cracked up, me spewing the mouthful of beer I'd foolishly started while pretending to be cool. Things were back to normal.

By the time we'd spent our weekly allowance of beer money, Jess had gotten the whole story, with all the personal details that only a best friend could appreciate. Curly signaled to the taxi guy who hung around for just such occasions, and we were driven to our respective homes. It was a good time to take a Sunday off.

CHAPTER 8

SLEEPING UNTIL 11:00, a breakfast of toasted bagel smothered with peanut butter, and two Tylenol with a tumbler of orange juice did the job on my hangover. Then Rover and I walked downtown to get my Jeep, picking a bouquet of wildflowers along the way. Back home, I put two cups worth in the Mr. Coffee. While it brewed, I took an empty mayonnaise jar out of the recycling and scraped off the label (someday, I should get a real vase). I put the flowers in water, poured a mug of coffee and grabbed my cell phone.

Some Sundays I call my folks. Mom and Dad are always home then, maybe watching a ball game or playing pinochle with the next-door neighbor. They love to hear from me, and never, ever give me shit for not calling for weeks. They never give me shit for anything. The worst I ever got that even came close to a lecture was, "Just make sure you have enough money in your pocket to call us if you need to."

"Hi, Mom. I'm not interrupting anything, am I?"

"Of course not. What could there be to interrupt? Harvey just dropped by, and we're about to start a game of cards, but I'd rather talk to you." She muffled the phone for a moment. "It's your youngest. Okay, I'll tell her," and back to me, "Your dad says hello. Harvey too. What's going on? Are you calling from Eden Beach?"

"Yeah, I'm home, doing nothing. Just thought I'd better check up on you guys, make sure you hadn't left town without leaving a forwarding address."

Mom laughed. "No, not yet. And you know if we do you'll be the first we tell. So, how are you, Lainey? Still caddying, aren't you? Do you have enough money to eat right?"

Mom's main concern was always that I might be starving. Which, if she'd thought about it, she'd know would never happen. Why? Because before I'm reduced to the level of eating out of garbage cans, I'd use the money in my pocket to phone home.

"I'm fine, Mom, still caddying, still making enough money, and still eating. In fact, I went to a really fancy Italian restaurant last night with a friend, and I think I gained five pounds."

"Oh how nice. Who were you with? Is he nice?"

Leave it to Mom to pick right up on it. She had radar for knowing when I was seeing a new guy. To be honest, that's probably why I called her today. A little boost of confidence from my biggest fan couldn't hurt. So I told her about Grant, even let her know that I was a little nervous about what I was feeling.

"But anyway, don't worry Mom. I'm not going to move too fast with this guy."

"Oh, I'm not worried at all, Lainey..." Then she gave me her oft-repeated and best guidance, "... as long as you're having fun."

I spent the rest of the day going to the Laundromat, the grocery store, and straightening up around the house. I usually waited until I had zero food (sorry Mom) and no clean clothes and the house had science projects growing in every corner before I took action. But today I enjoyed catching up on my chores at a leisurely pace. I placed the jar of flowers on the fish box/coffee table and stood back to take a look. My whole world was bright and cheery.

That observation made the hair on the back of my neck stand up, sent me to the fridge to get a beer, and sat me down on the just-vacuumed couch. I put my feet up on the fish box, careful not to knock over the flowers, and asked Rover, "Is this the true meaning of happiness?"

Rover, who thinks any question asked of him translates in Dog to "Do you want to jump up?" jumped up and curled next to me.

"Rover, what is wrong with this picture? This is too weird. We should be out driving around looking for something to do. Going to Jessica's, finding a party, shooting pool at Pappy's."

He raised his eyelids a smidge and puffed air out of his nostrils.

"No. You're right. This is cool. Hell, one day of domesticity isn't going to kill me, I guess. Not to worry."

I worked on my beer for another few quiet moments, then had a thought. This mood called for a little reflection, and I knew just where to look. While vacuuming earlier, I'd purposely ignored the grungy canvas duffle in the back of the

68

closet. I'd used it on the fishing trip and it still had a tinge of fish and diesel fumes. Inside, discarded and forgotten for over two months, was the black fabric-covered journal that I'd kept in those sorry ten days on the boat. If ever there was a time to read this crap, it was now. Maybe I could gain some perspective by learning from my mistakes.

I microwaved a mound of the deli mac-and-cheese I'd brought home from the grocery store, and opened the container of coleslaw. That was as close to a real dinner as I ever got for myself. I sat at the kitchen table with my plate and a fresh beer, opened the journal, and I dug in.

THURSDAY –

Last night was my first night at sea. I didn't believe we'd leave so late in the day, so Bobby caught me off guard. That was probably the best way it could've happened – quick before I had a chance to change my mind. I guess it is kind of a spooky idea, a woman who's a relative beginner with boats working as a boatpuller for the whole season in California with some guy she only knows from the bars. But I have day-fished with him and he seems to know what he's doing (as if I could tell) and all the other fishermen I know say his boat is in good shape. They said his craziness is just for town; when he's fishing he's okay. I like Bobby alright, at least I trust him not to get any ideas about our "working relationship." If there's one thing I can handle it's keeping it cool with the men I want to keep it cool with. Even his dippy wife Shelly trusted us to go together, not that he valued her opinion any. I guess that's who I'm replacing. She wants (or he wants her) to stay in Eden this season and have her baby, so

Bobby offered the job to me. He knows no guy would do it because all he uses a "boatpuller" for is to cook and clean for him. Of the three boats I've worked on, not one skipper has let me pull a fish like a boatpuller is supposed to do. Just clean 'em and steer the boat. And the Crapshoot *doesn't even need to be steered when she's trawling because she's got something called an "iron mike" that keeps her on course. But what the hell? I love the ocean, there's sure nothing keeping me in town, and I need a good adventure! Besides, he let me bring my dog.*

When we left Eden, everybody was at the jetty seeing us off. After Bobby had come to tell me we'd be leaving in an hour, I swung by the tavern to say goodbye. My drinking buddy, Jessica, was working but she got someone to watch the bar for her and she rounded up a bunch of folks to go to the jetty and wave to me. She walked all the way out to the very end of the jetty and I just know she stayed there watching us go until we were out of sight. There I was going off to seek my fortune and there was my very best friend and just about the whole town wishing me luck. It was a great feeling and I stood there waving back at them from the deck, taking it all in until Bobby yelled at me to get inside the wheelhouse and close the door before I got swept overboard.

Crossing the bar was pretty rough, but we didn't have any problem. The sun was down by the time we were out and it took me awhile to get used to the rolling. The Crapshoot *is a 45-footer and real sound, but before this I had only been out in the daytime when I could look at the horizon to keep from getting queasy. It gets so dark out there, stars are the only thing you can fix your eyes on. And there are so many! It felt like we were*

*in outer space – just propelling along through the voids on our
way to another planet.*

*Bobby had brought along his cousin Stanley, a kid about
fifteen, who had been helping Bobby work on the boat and was
going with us as far as Crescent City where he lives with his
folks. I was glad he was along because then it didn't look so bad
for me to crash out early when he did too. Bobby stayed awake
all night. We went real slow, waiting for his "running partners"
to catch up. They're two guys who harbor north of us and want
to fish California too. Bobby figured it would take them about
an hour, but we got to Cape Blanco before we even heard from
them on the radio. Our fathometer was on the blink, I mean
belly up (gotta start using fishing lingo) and I was scared for us
to go it alone, but I didn't say anything. Anyway, Bobby waited
for Conrad on the Gypsy to pass us and we went on with Joey
running somewhere behind us, but we couldn't see his lights.
The Gypsy is a little bigger boat than the Crapshoot, Bobby told
me, but Conrad was kind of a loner and never hired a crew.
Joey's boat, the Dixie, is too small for two people to sleep on so
Joey was alone too. I'd seen the Dixie, a double-ender that rolled
more than any boat I'd ever seen before, and I was glad to not
be on her.*

*When I woke up and saw daylight, we were just rounding
Point St. George and turning toward the Crescent City bar. It
was a good sleep. I had forgotten what a peaceful rocking
motion you feel out there with your eyes closed. Rover did fine.
At first I had put him down in the hull where I bunked but he
crawled under the covers and shook and cried. So I put him up
in the cabin and he slept on Stanley in the small bunk that
would later be mine. Good thing he's not very big (Rover, not*

Stanley). Anyway, today he's hopping in and out of the boat and running around the docks feeling pretty hot shit – a real boat dog.

Bobby and Conrad figure Joey must have taken a nap somewhere and lost us. We already went to eat breakfast at some restaurant here at the boat basin and he isn't in yet. Those guys are crashed and Stanley went home, so Rover and I are just loafing around the boat. Feels good.

Here comes Joey! I'm going to go help him dock.

FRIDAY –

My adventurous spirit was aroused again this morning with Conrad banging on the side of the wheelhouse and yelling, "What do you think you are, a banker?" to wake us up at 6:15 a.m. I thought, cool! After a day of doing nothing we were finally getting busy. All we did yesterday was dock the boats, sleep, and sit around bullshitting. I suppose these guys had needed a day to catch up since they'd stayed awake all night on the trip down.

Well, my first job as boatpuller was to fix breakfast and clean up for three stupid fishermen. What crap. The two others brought their contributions of food over to Conrad's boat, sat down at the table with their coffee and waited for me to serve them. I'm not sure whether I was actually told to cook or it was an unspoken demand that I gave in to just to be a nice guy. The rest of the morning I spent scrubbing and painting the Crapshoot *while the three men wandered the docks or sat around their respective boats doing what they told me was the "hard part" – thinking. I don't know if it's because I'm crew, or because I'm female. Either way it sucks.*

72

Half a day and a case of beer later, I and my shitfaced skipper went to Greg's house for showers. He's a local fisherman and an old friend of Bobby's – a real nice guy about 30, two kids, no wife, and good-looking. Thank goodness for a shower! The comforts of a house were awfully appealing and it's only been two days. Christ, I'll never make it.

Joey had gone over to his brother Mac's house and we were all expected to go there for dinner. I guess it was like a reunion for Joey and Mac because they hadn't seen each other since the beginning of last fishing season. Greg and kids headed on over and he let me use his truck to drive back to the docks to get Conrad, bring him back to Greg's house to get cleaned up, collect Bobby and then try to get both drunks to Mac's before dinner. It was pathetic. First I'm their cook and housekeeper, now I was their nursemaid. Mac's poor wife was in an even worse situation; she had a whole crew of them on her hands. She was trying to barbecue hamburgers and get salads and relishes ready when the men and kids were ready – not an easy task.

By the time Bobby, Conrad and I got there, she had lost whatever help she had from Mac because he and Joey were rivaling each other in beer-guzzling and bullshit. It looked like good ol' Greg was in charge of kids – his two and Mac's three – but most of the time they were running from one end of the house to the other, hollering orders for hamburgers at Mac's wife. (You know, I never did learn Mac's wife's name, or get a chance to talk to her. I'm sure she didn't think much of me – just another fucking fisherman.)

Trying to help, I dished up a plate of food for Conrad and sat him down. Then I heard Bobby yelling at me from the living room to get his too, but I ignored him. Boy, did that piss him off. Too bad, buddy. Enough's enough. I quit waitress work to go fishing, not wait on drunk fishermen.

After dinner we left all the kids with Mac's Poor Wife and went to town. I really felt privileged then – included in the fun and not left behind to clean up. Joey, Conrad, Greg, Mac, Bobby, and me. Just one of the guys. I shot some pool, drank some more, and came back to the boat aching and sunburnt, full of food and beer.

I just came back from a walk to the bathroom where I was surprised to find a pay phone I hadn't noticed before. Nice to know that somebody recognizes there are people still without cell phones, or with cheapo service plans, like me. I called the only number I could remember, Pappy's Tavern. I wanted to talk to Jessica but she wasn't there, and whoever it was who answered didn't know her number. So I left the message that I had called but it wasn't important.

One funny thing that Conrad said today – he wished a dragon or a sea monster would eat him and his boat so he "wouldn't have to fish no more."

SATURDAY —

Today started like yesterday, only I'm catching on; it was at least a couple of hours before I fixed breakfast. This time on Bobby's boat instead of Conrad's. It was rough. The mess facilities compare like a greasy spoon to fine dining. Maybe they're trying to punish me. Then, after clean-up, without a word of thanks or a "boy, that was good," it's back to the scrubbing and painting. I feel the temptation to bolt, but I can't quit until I see some money, and that doesn't come until the fish do.

After I finished what Bobby had told me to do on the boat, I sneaked over to the Gypsy and hung out with Conrad and some men who were drinking with him. Conrad is a very relaxed kind of guy, reminds me of an old hippie. After a while, the other men left and we sat and talked and he showed me around his boat. It's pretty fancy, even has a TV. I felt surprisingly comfortable with Conrad – not that I think that every fisherman is going to jump me if they get the chance, it's just that they tease and intimidate so much when they're together. I never suspected Conrad to be such a sweetheart.

I like Joey, too. He has an edgy sense of humor that I'm not too sure how to take sometimes, but after seeing how he lives, I can almost understand it. He's not as philosophical as Conrad, but quiet just the same, always watching. When he does say something, you get the feeling that there might be hidden intent. Like today, I was passing by where he was working on the Dixie and he tossed over a 300-yard mess of fishing line and told me to untangle it for him. I told him to go fuck himself. He said if he had told Bobby's wife, Shelly, to do it, she would have. I think that was a compliment.

It's annoying being compared to her and the other floozies who fished with Bobby. People see me with him and think I must be just the same. Disgusting. These horny fishermen should get their dicks slammed in their hatches.

Gotta go – Greg is here and Chrissie and Sean, his kids, are up in the parking lot waiting for me to come fly kites with them. I think we're going to their house for dinner tonight. I'd rather sleep.

LATER THAT NIGHT —

We got both kites up and it was really fun. They're good kids and seem like they miss having a woman around. I don't know what happened to their mom but it's none of my business. Joey, Bobby and I went to Greg's for showers and food and I had a good time. Greg is so adorable; it's hard to believe he's a fisherman.

A funny thing that happened – well, at least funny to Joey; he's very amused by Rover's cute-poufy-dog exterior and fierce, badass ego. So Joey, stoned out of his mind, sicked Rover on Greg's cat, yelling, "Get him, Killer!" That started Chrissie screaming her head off and Sean running after them yelling, "Get him, Killer! Get him, Killer!" Rover chased the poor cat around the house a couple of times, knocking over furniture and sliding his little legs on the linoleum, before they finally ran outside and the cat jumped a fence. The whole thing took maybe a minute, but Joey was still laughing later when we dropped him off at Mac's.

Bobby went downtown and I got left here at the boat. It's peaceful. It's only 8:00 on a Saturday night, and I'm ready for a quiet evening of reading, watching a great sunset over the harbor, maybe some TV with Conrad, and then SLEEP!

MONDAY —

Yesterday was hell.

It started mellow enough – I managed to sneak around, disappearing at the right times, without making breakfast. Joey had us over for tuna sandwiches about noon, then I worked as usual. Bobby messed with the engine. Then Conrad and Bobby decided we'd go over to the basin restaurant for dinner, so we got a ride with some maniac named Harry. To my surprise, we made it there alive, and then Bobby accidentally shut my foot in the door of the truck as I was getting out. It hurt like a sonofabitch, but I carried on like a trooper.

At the restaurant, I got another taste of the fisherman's sense of humor. Bobby secretly unscrewed the lid on the pepper shaker so that when Conrad went to use it – splaat! Well, Conrad thought that was so funny that he cleverly did the same thing to Bobby with the salt. It was a mess. I've never felt so feeble about not being able to afford a tip.

Back at the boats, we watched some TV and then Bobby went to town with Maniac Harry, and I took my sore foot to bed.

First Intrusion: Bobby wakes me up and tells me to give him $100 of his money that he had asked me to hold for him at the start of the trip. (Looking back, I see now what a tip-off that was that I was going out to sea with a loser, but I was starry-eyed at the time.) He's drunk but I want to go back to sleep so I give him the money. He says not to worry.

Second Intrusion: (this one lasting over an hour, starting about 3:00 a.m.) Bobby is back, telling me that part of a boatpuller's job is to wake up and bullshit with the drunk skipper any time of the night. I say, "Fuck off." Impossible to sleep, I listen to him tell me about my "duties" and about how easy he's been on me. I try to explain about wanting to be a boatpuller, not a nanny. Forget it, he doesn't hear me. He goes on saying part of fishing is jacking your buddies around. Like the pepper trick. I say, "You can have it." Then the topic turns to going out to sea with a drunk skipper. He tells me to check with Conrad on how cool it is. They all know this ocean so well they could make the trip with their eyes closed. I shudder. Finally, after I refuse to talk to him anymore, he leaves to go yank Joey and Conrad out of bed. Literally.

This morning, wonder of wonders! Joey woke me up for breakfast on the table at Conrad's. Alright! They cussed Bobby out for his crazy drunk shit, and I started feeling that maybe I was not alone. I asked about going out with a drunk at the wheel. Conrad shucked and jived, and Joey said it depended on the circumstances. In the clinches, it seems, the Brotherhood sticks together.

Oh well, I guess I'll find out when the time comes. Could be tomorrow – looks like we're going fishing.

I may be fishing for a new job.

CHAPTER 9

MY CELL PHONE buzzed from where I'd left it on the fish box, scaring the bejeezus out of me. I moved to answer it before it could buzz again, but I didn't recognize the number on the display.

"Hello?"

"Lainey, hi. It's Grant."

"Grant. Wow. Hi." A surprised laugh escaped my mouth.

"Am I interrupting anything?"

"What's there to interrupt? I don't even have a next-door neighbor who plays pinochle."

"What?"

"Nothing. Sorry, just an old family joke."

"I should meet your family."

"Now you're joking. So how are things in Seattle?"

"Same. I just left the office, heading back to my condo after a very long two days. I was thinking about you. I was wishing that I'd been able to stay in Eden longer."

"Yeah, me too." Uncomfortable pause. "I mean, it seemed like you had a couple of good days on the golf course."

"I had a great time. The best time I've had in... in I don't even remember when. And you were the best thing about it. I wanted to tell you that, in case I didn't say it. I don't know what I said when I left. I was in sort of a daze, I think."

"You were? A daze?" Was that a good thing?

"Well, I do remember that you had a goofy smile on your face after I kissed you. I remember that clearly."

"Was that after the first kiss or the second?"

"Both, I think. Yeah, both. I remember the kisses, your smile, and the way I knew that I'd have an embarrassing situation if I didn't leave when I did. I remember that like it was the day before yesterday."

"It *was* the day before yesterday." I giggled. How was it that this guy could make me actually giggle?

"Ah – there it is. That magical sound that can turn downtown traffic into a beautiful day on the Oregon coast."

"Hey, I don't want to distract you if you're driving."

"No, you're not. Just pulled into the parking garage. Give me all the distractions you can. Like, what were you doing right before I called?"

My mind had to warp light-years back to that century I was in before I answered my phone. Talk about a one-eighty.

"I can't tell you. The excitement might attract unwanted attention in your parking garage."

"Oh, so you know my garage. Okay, don't tell me. But what about in the past two days? Anything exciting? Like, have you met anyone who, well... this sounds so lame... who takes your mind off me?"

"No, no matter how hard I try." I took a power breath. "Grant, I'm going to be honest with you. This is scary. I'm just starting with this caddie thing and I don't want to blow it. But if it even looks like I'm one of those seasonal sluts who are just here for the bucks, I'm finished. I'd never be taken seriously again. It only takes a whisper of a rumor to make it so." I took another breath.

"I want to make this job last. It might be the only opportunity I have that can give me some real roots. And even though an affair with you would be amazing, I have to pass if you're really just another fucking golfer."

Oh my god. Did I just say that? Gulp.

"I'm sorry, Grant. I didn't mean to call you..."

"Hey, it's okay. You're absolutely right. You just met me. How would you know I'm not one of those stupid creeps?"

His tone was more understanding than defensive, so I calmed down.

"No, I know you're not a creep. You're really a nice guy, and I like you and all. But do you know what I mean, about my worries if I go out with you?"

"I do, and I appreciate that you told me. But there is something I want to tell you. This is hard, because I don't like to talk about myself. I wish I could say this face-to-face, so I could read your eyes."

"You're doing fine. I'm listening."

"It's this. I'm twenty-eight years old and I haven't had many relationships. The ones I have had I screwed up because I wasn't paying attention. This isn't something I'm proud of. I'm a workaholic, or at least I was. I'm learning to relax now, and although I wasn't looking for a woman in my life, I think I

81

could handle it... I mean her... I mean you. Handle isn't a good word, is it?"

"I get your point. Keep going."

"Okay. Lainey, you challenge me, you make me pay attention. And that's a good thing. You're also fun, you're witty, and..."

"Don't forget cute as hell."

"Not just cute, you're smokin'."

"Whoa. Get serious."

"I am. You don't know how hard it was for me to keep my eyes off you on the golf course, in your cute little jumpsuit. Hot, I'm telling you."

"You're weird."

"Lainey, I can seriously say that I've never met anyone like you. You've managed to mess my head up so much that for the past two days the guys I work with were worried about me. They said I'm being nice.

"So, here's the deal. I am not giving up on showing you that I'm serious. A client of mine wants to go to Singing Bluffs because, when I told him about it he freaked. He's dying to go, and he's taking me along. We'll be there this Friday. After our round I'll come get you and we'll go out, have another nice dinner or a walk on the beach or whatever you want. We can show ourselves in public or hide behind closed doors if you want. Hell, I'll wear a disguise if that's what it takes."

"This Friday? What will happen at the Bluffs? It would be kind of... uh, awkward if I caddied for you. How would that work? I mean, you'd be paying me. And the tip! Oh, no, you can't tip me. How weird would that be?"

"Lainey, slow down. You can caddie for me or not, whatever you say. But I can't imagine golfing without you. That wouldn't be any fun at all. I don't think there'll be a problem."

"I don't know. It's never come up before. I'll have to think about it." The thought of caddying for someone else while knowing Grant was golfing somewhere on the course with another caddie made me queasy. "Anyway, I'm glad you're coming. I'll try to not be so nervous."

"And you'll go out with me? Maybe show me more of Eden, meet some of your friends? Hey, maybe we can go to Pappy's."

"Oh god. Let me think about that one, too. Remember, you're kind of new at this relationship thing. You might not want to subject yourself to my friends yet."

"Okay. Wow, this is so cool. Now I'm really excited. But I'm freezing my butt off in this garage. Lainey, I've got to go. Is it okay if I call you tomorrow night?"

"Yeah, sure. I'd like that. I promise I'll keep my cell handy. Actually, I'm not very good at that, so keep trying if I don't answer right away."

"Oh, you can count on it. Bye, Lainey. You made my day. Talk to you tomorrow. Bye."

"Bye, Grant."

Wow. That was mind-blowing. I sat motionless at my tiny kitchen table, feeling the need to look around me for a reality check. Yep, it's my cozy little house, and there's my cozy little dog sleeping on my cozy little couch.

I looked at my cell phone and saw that it was ten-thirty. I needed to shower and get to bed. Enough of this Prince Charming fairy tale stuff. He's just a guy, and I'm just going out on a couple of dates with him, talk on the phone once in a while, normal boy-girl stuff. No big deal, Tidwell, get your head out of the clouds.

Of course, I wasn't the least bit sleepy even after a long shower. I kept the reading light on and stared at the ceiling for a while wondering, *can I do this?*

There was no way I'd ever get to sleep without getting my mind off the question. So I retrieved the fishing-trip journal from the kitchen, and began where I'd left off.

TUESDAY –

The California fishing season opened today, and we missed it. Ironically, we all had hangovers except Bobby – he came home early last night.

A friend of his from Brookings came into town yesterday. His name is Ray and I sort of know him because he fished out of Eden last year and I became good friends with his wife while he was out. Of course, when you're with your fishing buddies, it's not cool to run into one of your wife's friends, so we didn't acknowledge each other. With him was a big, jolly, gray-haired guy named Jack who I liked right off. But I didn't get to talk to him much because they all went off to town.

That left me with nothing to do, so I offered to help Joey and Conrad work on their boats. They had me running errands for a while but it was pretty low-key. When they called it quits, Joey went off with Mac, and Conrad and I took the Gypsy *through the boat basin to the fisheries to take showers. There was only one so I went first, and the manager made a big deal about putting a sign on the door so that no guys would walk in on me.*

(Oh boy, breaking down the sex barriers again.) We took our time getting back, feeling refreshed and relaxed. Conrad taught me how his boat's radar worked, talking real plain, and again I felt that there might be something to this fishing business.

We caught up with Mac and Joey back at the docks and all headed for an evening on the town. We found Ray and Jack at the Turf Club, a dark, seedy, smoke-to-the-floor hard liquor bar, but Bobby had already gone back to the boat. Ah, freedom! Bobby and I had not spoken to each other all day and I was glad to avoid him.

Somebody bought a couple of rounds and I was having a good time, getting teased a lot but nothing too offensive. Then some local girls came in and the comments started getting raunchy, so I decided that was my cue to cut out. I whispered to the bartender that I was leaving and to tell them later that I had gone to the boat, and I slipped out unnoticed. A few blocks away I found a friendly-looking tavern called The Yankee Lady that looked more my speed. It turned out to be a little less than friendly when the bartender made me go back to the boat for my I.D.

Anyway, it wasn't a bad walk. Making sure not to wake Bobby, I got my I.D. and decided to take Rover along with me. He'd been real good about staying on the docks, but since I knew where I was going this time I figured he wouldn't be any trouble. He's an old street dog from way back, and good company. Along the way we bought a hamburger at the drive-in and shared it as we walked.

The Yankee Lady was a nice, mellow place, what the fishermen called a hippie bar. I drank my beers slowly to make them last and watched TV. No one paid me much attention, which was fine. I even started to leave once but changed my mind when I got outside and felt how cold it was. Having one more for the road, I recognized a guy I knew from my old hometown, Eureka. He sat with me for a while, asked how I was doing, and it was a shot in the arm to talk to someone I could relate to again. Then he gave me and Rover a ride to the docks on his Harley-Davidson and I hoped someone would see me. Guess I was feeling pretty loose and wanted those jerks I worked with to know I could get along alright without them.

Surprise! The boys' party had broken up, Ray was sleeping in the hull bunk with Bobby and big Jack had mine! I woke Bobby up and he told me Conrad had taken the Gypsy *to Brookings but I could sleep on the* Dixie *because Joey had gone to his brother's. So I tottered over to the* Dixie *and there's Joey on the top bunk of a double-decker, the only clear space available. In the dark it was hard to tell what all the clutter was, but I could see that it was close quarters. Being ready to pass out, I couldn't be choosy, so Rover and I sneaked into the bottom bunk that was piled with gear and tools. Joey's jacket was lying on the deck so I picked that up to use for my only covers.*

Bad night. Joey thought it was pretty funny when he woke up in the morning and found me curled up with my dog and all that junk and freezing to death. At least he gave me his blanket and let me sleep late. And Bobby didn't bother me all day. Conrad came back in the afternoon (I had been worried about him but no one else seemed to be) and we ate dinner on the Gypsy. *It seems he was feeling bar-bound last night and just had to get out. I think I know how he felt.*

Bobby wanted to test out the engine work he'd done so we fired her up and went out for a spin before dusk. It was beautiful. The sea was calm and the Crapshoot *rode smooth. Maybe we'll fish tomorrow. I'm ready.*

FRIDAY —

We've been fishing offshore Eureka for two days and we're belly up. It's really crazy. We got here Wednesday night, trawled all day yesterday and today and I think we've got seven legal salmon. It's the same story with Joey and Conrad. The three boats keep checking back and forth with each other on the "Mickey Mouse" (that's what they call their radios – I guess because they're not very efficient but I don't know for sure because no one will give me a straight answer). The other two are right around here somewhere but we can't see them because of the fog. It's cold and gray and choppy as hell out here and it seems to me that we're wasting more fuel and bait than we're making money. Besides all that, I'm sick as a dog. I thought that hangover the other day was bad – but I've never felt so bad as this three-day seasickness.

But I'm doing my job, cooking for my skipper whenever he says he's hungry and cleaning fish whenever he pulls one. The rest of the time, he's out there at the stern knocking himself out pulling empty lines in, re-baiting, letting them back out, and I'm in here moaning in agony. It's almost killing me to know my parents' home is within 15 miles as the crow flies. I had thought for sure we'd head into the bay Wednesday night. What's the point of floundering around out here for nothing? If they're not running, they're not running. Either we move on to Ft. Bragg like he had planned in the first place or we go into Eureka and sit it out. Maybe my throwing up all the time is making me less perceptive, but I really don't get what's going on here.

I almost didn't leave Crescent City. Bobby wanted to cast off at 3:00 Wednesday morning and he was blind drunk. We had a hell of a confrontation and I finally talked him into sleeping a few hours first. Now I wish I had just let him go by himself.

My seasickness is offset only by the boredom. Every once in a while we hear another boat talking on the radio – all of them on their way somewhere else. (TAKE ME WITH YOU!) Or we can listen to Conrad tell us what's on TV. But I think the most entertaining is Joey cussing out the locals on shore talking on their CB's. One lady who's on all the time really gets mad at us for using swear words. She says her little boy loves to listen to the fishermen and she wishes they'd clean up their language. Joey had a lot of fun with that. I hope the lady's son has a good sense of humor.

There's all kinds of time to think about things out here. I've been thinking a lot about karma. I learned once that Eskimos always thank the spirit of the animal they kill to eat. Fishermen here seem to believe that everything out there is theirs for the taking, no homage needed. Every so often we see junk go floating by – plastic containers, beer cans, ruined slickers, gloves – and I realize other fishermen must have the same habit Bobby does of cleaning decks by throwing everything over-board. Shakers (small, illegal salmon) are left on the lines too long and ripped off the hooks when they're finally brought in, so that they float lifelessly away from the boat. Bottom fish that don't bring a price are left on the deck to dry out because they're nuisances that eat the bait meant for more profitable catch.

My skipper admits to having no fear, i.e., respect, for the ocean. He says he's unsinkable. He's pissed off at it right now, wondering why the ocean isn't feeding him.

SATURDAY —

I've been resting here at my folks' house. I hadn't decided to stay until we docked and I walked on dry land again. Then it just seemed the most natural thing to do. Rover agreed it was a pretty good idea. As soon as we got to the parking lot he ran over to some high grass and kicked and rolled in it. The poor guy. I think he found it rather distasteful to have to crap on the bow of the boat for three days.

I don't know what finally made the men decide to give up and turn into Humboldt Bay, but that ride was the prettiest I've ever seen. My nausea went away as soon as we crossed the bar. Bobby was quietly resigned to Joey's and Conrad's plan of waiting a few days in Eureka, and he didn't think twice about paying me off and letting me go. He got his remaining cash back from me and we were even. The three guys gave me a lot of shit about getting sick in the first bad sea and going belly up; I'm sure the story will get back to Eden before I do.

So, after a farewell drink with the boys at the Vista Del Mar, the harbor dive more commonly known as the VD, I took my share of the catch – a crummy eighty bucks – plus a couple of shakers and I called my dad to come get me.

At first I was worried about people being disappointed in my quitting the boat. I expect a few "I-told-you-so"s and cracks because I'm not as tough as I thought I was. But I'm glad it's over. The whole schmucky business – the men and the bars and the fish plants – everything. While selling our fish I thought of asking the manager if I could catch a ride north on the fish truck this week. But after all the back-slapping friendliness he'd shown me when I was with three smelly fishermen and a hundred pounds of fish, I got the feeling the creep wouldn't even talk to me if he couldn't make a buck out of it. And I didn't want to deal.

When Dad brought me home with my gear and my dog, I felt such an overwhelming sense of calm, of having my fate in my own hands again. I sat and talked with my folks about my experience for a while, took a long shower, then scaled and wrapped the shakers with Dad. Mom and Dad understood why I quit and that made me feel more at ease with myself again. Dad's feelings had been a concern to me, because with no sons, anything I do that is unusual for a girl is exciting for him. He was only disappointed that the fishing wasn't what I had expected. Mom just said that she had stopped worrying about me years ago (openly anyway) and knew that I knew what was best for me. She listened to my story empathetically and, with only slightly-forced confidence, assured me that it wouldn't be long before I found another adventure.

I SET THE journal on the nightstand, said good night to Rover, and as I turned out the light I wondered what Mom knew that I didn't know.

90

CHAPTER 10

GETTING UP AND going to work on Monday morning was different. I felt like one of those regular working stiffs who, after a relaxing Sunday, was now having trouble making the adjustment. My non-traditional job usually meant going to work day after day, after day, for as long as I could stand it. Because it was June, the high season at the Bluffs, most caddies showed up every day. Of course, rookies couldn't be certain that they'd get a bag, but we showed up anyway. While doing our time in the bucket, eagerness counted.

But my weekend player hadn't stayed through Sunday, so it wasn't out of the ordinary for me to take that day off. Now here I was, driving the eleven miles from my house to the resort, sharing the highway with commuting carpoolers, delivery trucks, and contractors' pickups.

I wondered what Monday morning traffic was like in downtown Seattle.

The shack was buzzing at 6:30, and I barely had a moment to suit up before Larson called my name. The sky had that anything-could-happen look to it, so although we wore our whites, caddies needed their blue rainproof coveralls handy. I stuffed mine and extra socks, gloves, and towels into a pack that I could put in a golf bag without the guest's objection, and hustled to the staging area. Tucson Johnny and Tick were ahead of me, already chatting with the Hollows starter, Kelly, at the curtain doorway. She bounced on the toes of her sneakers like a horse at the starting gate. Kelly's energy was contagious, and her obvious love affair with her job gave me an optimistic outlook for the day, despite the weather.

Then I turned to see the caddie trailing me and almost peed my pants. The bloodshot, dark-circled, flinty eyes that I looked into couldn't be helped by any amount of mascara. Her face was a train wreck, and there was something about her posture and movement that said ol'-cowpoke. I thought of the rode-hard-and-put-away-wet joke, but stifled it.

After recovering, I said, "Hi. I'm Lainey. It's Starla, isn't it?"

I put out my hand. She ignored it, and as she brushed past me I noticed that there was absolutely no life in her eyes. I think I felt my soul start to leave my body.

"Okay then. Is it Twila? Give me a hint." I followed her to the curtain, not liking the sudden turn my outlook was taking.

"Howdy, Lainey," Tucson Johnny said. "Howdy, Twila."

Twila it is then. How will I remember? Let's see, Twila, like twilight, as in end of day, as in darkness, as in end of life as we know it. Got it.

Tick nodded his head a half-inch in greeting and then the shuttle pulled up. We met the players, four middle-aged boys' club types who didn't look fit enough to walk a full loop. I had the distinct feeling it was going to be a slow day. Kelly gave her spiel about pace of play, spoke into her radio, and we were off.

My dude was Mr. Cutlass from Bend, who had a buzz cut that had Far Right Conservative written all over it. While we walked to the first tee, he did nothing but talk about how much better the resorts were in Bend.

How nice for you, you fat windbag. Why didn't you stay there to play?

I said instead, "Nice. Maybe I'll get a chance to go there sometime." When I saw the creepy leer that Cutlass shot me and realized how my words could be misinterpreted, I added, "I'll be sure to tell my boyfriend about your recommendation. Maybe he'll take me."

So what if it was a cop-out? It was the only thing I could think of. The dressing-down Tiny Sue got in the manager's office had me worried. Where was the middle ground? I considered who I was dealing with – a know-it-all redneck loudmouth who undoubtedly expected more than the usual caddie services from a chick. He wouldn't think twice about complaining that I was too standoffish. I decided to double down.

"My boyfriend isn't big on golf though. He's more into bodybuilding, football, wrestling, that kind of thing. So, what will it be, Mr. Cutlass, your driver or your wood?"

The day passed with only a few dark clouds. Although I worked my tail off, things went okay. I had a little fun pushing Cutlass. He was trying so hard not to be shown up by a little girl carrying a big bag, that I upped my pace just to watch him sweat. He tipped me $50 which, for a Conservative, is better than decent. And I bet I even got a good rating out of him. My boyfriend would be proud.

Twila, on the other hand, must have ended up with more than a hundred bucks in her pocket. Her nonstop slinking and strutting was so gross, I couldn't believe that the fool she was bagging for didn't know she was playing him. Judging by how the other three were drooling, I guess for some guys the golf course becomes a high-priced meat market if your caddie is a ho. Johnny and Tick, however, showed that they were not only good caddies, they were good role models. While Twila was giving me the willies, they were giving me the lessons that I needed.

For example, on the No. 17 tee box, which steps the golfer up to a fantastic view of the Pacific and miles of surf-lined beach, our boys were jockeying for position to be first in line to hire Twila for tomorrow.

"Embrace her, gentlemen," Johnny said. "She's a pleasure there for the taking."

Everybody except Tick, who silently studied the scorecard, looked at Johnny with varying degrees of embarrassment. Johnny stood next to his dropped golf bag with arms outstretched, facing the ocean and with an unmistakable gleam in his eye.

"No matter how many times I see it, Mother Nature grabs me by the balls and takes my ever-lovin' breath away with this view. Her gifts don't get any better than this, do they, gentlemen? I mean, now I ask you."

I didn't need more than that. The previous night's review of my shitty fishing trip, the phone call with Grant, followed by a fairly good day at the office – I was feeling better and better about my life.

IT RAINED ON and off for three days. The only good thing about June rains on the Oregon coast is that the nasty north wind doesn't blow as hard as usual. You either get downpours with a light wind, or clear sky and freaking cold Northerlies. The Bluffs had a bunch of cancellations. By Thursday, Grant's client who wanted to bring him down for a weekend of golf had changed his mind three times. Grant said he was a real nice guy, but kind of a wuss.

Each day, the shack was crowded and we suffered hours of waiting with no guarantee of an assignment. Two days in a row I was skipped over. If it hadn't been for Tiny Sue, the boredom would've been intolerable. She was still being punished, she said, and was one of the first ones scratched when players canceled. I felt bad for her, but having her to talk to while we waited was a treat. Finally I had someone to swap stories with, stories only girl caddies, *nice* girl caddies, could appreciate. And I learned a few tricks of the trade, like how to help your player avoid an onset of the dreaded yips.

"It happens mostly with short putts, but long putts or chips can do it to you too," Sue explained. "There's a buildup of negative expectation as you approach the dance floor – you begin to expect to miss, and you do. I've seen players go from Ben Hogan to Hulk Hogan in a hurry, so I've learned to watch for it. When he hands me the club he used on the approach, I take a look into the guy's eyes. If they're kinda glassy – you know that deranged look? – and beads of sweat are popping out on his forehead, it's time for distraction strategies. Like, say something nice about his clubs. They love to show off a good set of sticks. While he's bragging about his irons, you're building his confidence and he's forgotten all about that putt coming up."

"Cool," I said. Look for deranged eyes. Sure, I could do that.

"Of course, the yips are really just a lack of practicing, repeating the mechanics of a sound stroke. And here's another thing – if the dude is some cocky asshole, I tell him, 'Just swing the club at the target. There's only two things that can happen – you make it or you miss it. At least we know you won't lose the ball.' That usually snaps him out of it."

Another bonus of having Sue to hang out with was that Rocks left me alone. Now there's the trick I really need to learn, how to make Rocks fear me like he fears Tiny Sue. He and his posse were around, but they kept their distance and I didn't hear one wiseass remark. And I didn't run into him at Pappy's either, because I stayed home. It was a nice break.

On Thursday forecasters had called for 100% chance of rain, so out-of-towners had canceled earlier in the week. But it turned out to be a gorgeous day and the shack was full of caddies rarin' to go. There was a steady stream of tee times set for both courses, but they were mostly locals. Some local duffers like to take advantage of slow days at the resort, but they use pull carts instead of caddies. In the high season the $275 greens fees alone are too steep for most locals. Add on the $50 caddie fee, a frugal $25 gratuity, and Eden's humble retirees are having heart attacks before they've even teed off.

At 2:00 I decided to call it a day. The sunshine drew me to the beach, me and a couple dozen other people. I had to put

96

Rover on a leash to be polite (and legal) because there were kids and dogs all over the place. The waves were low and mild, the deceptive appearance of a So-Cal beach. I watched tourist kids running and jumping in the freezing cold water, with their oblivious parents sitting yards away up on the dry sand. Kids squealed, dogs barked. I hated to spoil their fun by telling them about the dangerous undertow and sneaker waves that our beaches are known for. So I kept quiet, checked my cell phone for signal strength, and continued walking. Neither Rover nor I were crazy enough to make any heroic efforts and go in after someone, but I would be the first to call for help.

I'd no sooner put my phone back in my pocket when I felt it vibrate. The caller ID displayed GG, the code I now had, after three evening phone calls, programmed for Grant's cell number.

"Hey! Hi, Grant."

"Hi, Lainey. Busy?"

"Terribly. There's a bunch of stupid kids playing in the ocean and Rover and I are on lifeguard duty. But what the hell. If the idiot parents don't care when their kid gets pulled out to sea, why should I? Where are you calling from?"

"From the office. You're on the beach? Wow, how lucky can you get! Did you get an early loop?"

"No. It was a slow day. Again."

"Oh, I'm sorry. Tomorrow you'll work, wait and see."

"What makes you so sure?"

"Because I know of at least one guest who will request Lainey Tidwell to caddie for him and will accept no others."

"Oh yeah? Who's that?"

"You'll never guess. Scott changed his mind again and we're flying down in the morning. We'll be at the resort by nine, nine-thirty, and our tee time is scheduled for ten."

"Really? Are you sure? The last time we talked you told me he chickened out because he didn't like the weather," I said, looking up at the clear blue sky.

"Yeah, I know. But his wife talked him into it. She called him a pansy-ass."

"Nothing like girl power to shame a guy into doing something. How old is this guy, and how come he wants to treat you to a golf trip, anyway?"

"Mid-thirties, and because he thinks I'm a great property manager. His family has owned a block of prime real estate overlooking Elliot Bay for generations. When Scott inherited it, he put a lot of money into renovations and it paid off. I met him when I was starting up my business three years ago and I've managed his properties ever since. He treats me well because I keep his buildings occupied and maintained. The money keeps coming in."

"So you're good at what you do."

"That's what I've been telling you. Now, here's what we can do. Scott will request you as his caddie, on my recommendation, and I'll carry my own bag. We'll have a good round of golf, you'll earn a fee plus a fat tip because Scott will love you..."

"... because I'm good at what I do."

"Yes you are. And the best part is I get to spend a day with you without *you* having to worry about improprieties. Sound good?"

"I guess so." As excited as I was to see Grant again, I couldn't let go of the feeling that things were moving too fast. "Did you say ten o'clock tee time?"

"Right. Don't sound so thrilled."

"No, no. I really am. It's just... oh, nothing. It'll be fine. Great, I mean."

"I make you nervous, don't I?"

"A little."

"Just wait. Tomorrow will be a breeze. We'll talk and laugh, just like we've been doing on the phone, and you'll give me shit just like you did on the golf course the first day I met you."

"I did not!"

"Oh yeah, you did. And it was perfect. So relax and we'll have a good time. I can't wait to see you. Hey, did you decide where you want to go afterwards, on our *date*?"

We'd bantered this point around already in previous talks. How would I ever be able to go out with him without the whole caddie shack knowing about it? If Grant was trying to get me to relax, this wasn't the right topic to bring up.

"I don't know. I can't figure this whole thing out yet. Wait – will your friend Scott be with us?"

"No way. I'm not sharing you with him in the evening, too. He'll stay in his room and call his wife like the good boy that he is. You will be all mine."

For a moment the sound of the ocean faded away and I felt a flash of heat instead of the cold wind on my face.

"Okay," was all I could say.

"Lainey, don't worry. It'll all come together. I promise not to jeopardize your job or your reputation. For now, let's just talk. How's Rover?"

I'd almost forgotten the little bugger, peacefully trotting alongside me like a well-behaved pooch. This leash bit wasn't a bad idea.

CHAPTER 11

I GOT UP the next morning early enough to wash my hair and do what I could to file the rough edges of my fingernails. One of these days I should do as Jessica recommends and see what this manicure business is all about. I could probably do with a haircut, too. I took one last disappointing look in the mirror, jammed a Mariners cap on my head, and gave a quick goodbye–stay-home-and-be-good to Rover. I had just enough time to get to the shack and look relaxed for five minutes before Grant and his friend called for a caddie.

At 9:45 a full squad of caddies was already out on both courses, but there were still about fifty waiting to get a bag. When Larson called my name for the Bluffs, heads turned.

"Hold the phone," Rocks piped up. "What's the deal here? Since when does a first-year get a personal request from a guest this early in the season?"

"Since now," Larson said. "Be a big boy, Rocks, and don't get your panties in a twist. Tidwell's been doing a great job and guests are giving her good ratings. They recommend her to their friends. That's how it works. Take a lesson."

I hustled up-and-out with as much dignity as I could get away with, resisting the temptation to flip the bird at Rocks as I passed him.

Outside I managed a quick peek at my reflection in the window before scurrying off to the shuttle. I decided that the ball cap and Oakleys gave me a professional look. Now all I had to do was act like I knew what I was doing and impress the hell out of Grant's friend with my caddying expertise. No different from any other day. Except that I would be spending this day within sniffing distance of a very hot, fascinating, clever, funny – and did I say hot? – guy, who just so happened to be interested in me.

The shuttle dropped me off and I had time to BS with the new starter for a few minutes, a guy named Tyler with an enviable caffeine buzz. I'm sure I gave the appearance of nonchalance when I heard Grant's wolf whistle.

In my best Jersey accent I said, "You talkin' to me?"

"Well, I'm sure as hell not talking to this guy." Grant pumped Tyler's hand, but his eyes were on me. "Good morning. What a day! Is this a great day for golf, or what?"

"How do you do, sir," Tyler said, "and you're right about that. It is a good day for golf. Now, let's get you two started. Mr. Garner, I believe you are carrying your own bag, and Mr. Paulson, you requested that Lainey be your caddie today."

Scott Paulson was just about the most attractive rich guy who I'd ever shaken hands with. Mid-thirties, maybe, but the energy he put out would make college girls want to tap in.

I tore my eyes away just an instant to see that Grant was grinning like a madman.

"You know, Lainey, you're gonna want to give this guy way more help than you gave me. He's definitely going to need it."

"Hi, Lainey. Glad to meet you. And you think he's kidding, but he's absolutely right. I'm not the best golfer in the world, but I do like a good game." He shook my hand and his smile almost made me want to take him home and ask my mom if I could keep him.

"Nice to meet you, Mr. Paulson. I'll do my best to make sure you have a great round."

"Please call me Scott. I'm not *that* old," he laughed. "And it's sure spectacular so far."

Tyler recited the course introductory bit in less time than it usually took Kelly at the Hollows, and I thought *she* was hyper. Grant picked up his bag, I picked up Scott's and we were off. I could tell this was going to be a speedy game.

"What an amazing course! I can't believe this place," Scott said, nearly cuffing me when he threw his arms out to express himself adequately.

Grant slowed a bit so that I'd be matching step with him. "You should've seen his eyes bug out when we came in. We swung by the cabin to drop off our stuff, and it's a good thing I was driving. Scott would've driven us straight into a tree."

"Well, I know you told me that this place was in the woods, but I had no idea. I mean, the cabins are secluded! And then you come around a curve and there's this beautiful lodge, with the ocean in the background. We passed right by a family of five or six deer grazing away like they owned the place."

Scott must have picked up Tyler's buzz. He was talking a mile a minute, clearly blown away by the Bluffs, when we rounded the top of the knoll at the first tee box. The view of the coastline before us, just beyond the green, silenced him for a moment. Then he swore, loudly.

"Oh, I'm so sorry, Lainey. It just slipped out." He was getting red and I felt sorry for him.

"Don't worry about it. I've heard worse."

Grant rolled his eyes. "You've *said* worse." When I saw Scott's smile, I had a feeling that Grant might have talked up more than the resort's golf.

Ignoring my look of indignation, he flipped a tee in the air to determine who went first. The tee landed pointing at Scott, and Grant said, "Show me how you do it, Bubba. Grab your big stick and let 'er rip."

On the fairway we split away from Grant to follow Scott's hooked ball into the rough, and Scott got his first introduction to huckleberry bushes and beach grass. The course designers left a shitload of ball-devouring vegetation covering the links just to make the game more interesting, as if the gale-force winds weren't enough.

"Here it is, sir. I don't think you can play it though. Don't feel bad, you're still in good shape. That was a great drive and you're on the right side, so you have a good look at the green. If you take an unplayable from here, you can afford the stroke."

"Thanks," he said as I handed him the ball, "but call me Scott." He took a drop and hit a nice 8-iron to the fringe, not far from Grant's ball. As we walked ahead he asked me, "Have you been caddying long?"

104

"No, just started in April."

"Wow. You seem pretty good at it. Do you golf?"

"Not yet. I like watching and learning about the game more than I think I'd like playing."

"That's not something you hear every day. Good for you. Grant said you were smart."

I decided not to ask what else Grant had said about me. They both chipped on and two-putted, which left Scott trailing Grant by one. I noticed that neither was marking a score card.

"Do you want me to keep a card?" I asked because usually players like to keep their own.

"Nah," Grant said. "Thanks, but we never keep score when just the two of us play. It's more fun without dealing with those niggling little details."

They both laughed, and I knew this was going to be a fun day.

At the turn the guys went into the snack bar that the resort had tucked away behind the dunes to give players a break from the elements. Grant patted the bench next to him and motioned for me to join them. Okay, this happens sometimes – guests buy their caddies a soda and sit with them for a minute. I looked around nervously as I walked in. There were two other groups of players there, one threesome just leaving with two caddies I didn't know, and a foursome who, judging by their loudness, had been there awhile. I caught a glimpse of a couple caddies squatting on their haunches at the edge of the building, smoking cigarettes and peering inside impatiently.

One of the foursome stood and walked to the counter. He ordered a beer from the friendly retiree/bartender, then turned to Grant and Scott.

"You boys can go ahead and follow them out if you want. It seems we're taking a longer break than we planned," he said, punctuating with a gross burp.

"Hey, thanks," Scott said. "We're moving pretty fast, so we won't hold you up."

"No problem," said the burper, and he veered back to his pals.

I graciously declined Scott's offer of a hotdog, but accepted a Diet Pepsi. While they ate Grant and Scott talked excitedly about their favorite shots on the front nine. I sat attentively, like the professional I was, ready to prompt them when enough time had passed for the threesome ahead to have started for the green.

"I'll go up to the tee box and check ahead for you. Thanks again for the Pepsi, Mr. Paulson," I said, slipping my head and arm into the bag's straps.

As I hustled away I heard Grant say, "The 'Mr. Paulson' is for show. Don't worry. She'll go back to calling you Scott when we're out of earshot of co-workers. It's a code-of-ethics thing."

Scott said, "Ohh-kay." They chugged their beers and moved to catch up with me.

The rest of the day went so well, it hardly felt like work. My course-reading acumen was right on and my player couldn't have been nicer. Scott turned out to be a pretty good golfer, considering it was his first time on links like these, and he had the same sunny, casual attitude towards golf that Grant had. The three of us had a lot of laughs and I was sorry when it ended.

At the pro shop entrance I set down Scott's bag of shiny, clean clubs and turned to shake his hand with sincere gratitude. He smiled back and pressed some bills into my hand.

"It's been a real pleasure meeting you, Lainey. How about joining us again tomorrow? Grant says we should play Hemlock Hollows, just to get the full effect."

"Exactly. Right, Lainey? You just gotta play both courses to fully appreciate the beauty here. And Lainey is the best tour guide."

"Jeesh, Grant. You make it sound like I work for the Chamber of Commerce. Please ignore him, Scott, and I'd be glad to caddie for you again. I appreciate the request."

"Great. I'll go set up a tee time," Scott said. He went into the pro shop and I pocketed the fee plus tip without looking at it.

"See, I told you," Grant said. "Everything went great, and your virtuous reputation is still intact."

"It's early yet. We've still got to get through the next phase – our *date*."

"I can't wait," Grant said, flashing his irresistible eyes in a way that made my toes curl. "Go home, relax a while, and I'll come pick you up in, say, two hours? I'll take you wherever you want to go. I am here to serve at your pleasure," he said with a discreet bow.

I couldn't help but smile back at him. The thought of having him come to my house, to be there for *me*, obliterated the stupid logic that had me freaked out about being seen in public with him. I didn't feel the worry I'd had myself psyched up for. Also missing was the tiredness that I usually felt at the end of a loop, when my day ended up with a sad beer at Pappy's.

"Don't dress up," I told him. "We're going slumming."

ROVER AND I heard a car pull up in front of my house, and Rover immediately went into a frenzy as if recognizing a long-lost pal. The rental car wasn't even the same shape or color as the first time he'd seen him, so I don't know how he knew it was Grant.

"Cool it, Tazmo. It's just a guy. You act like I never have guys come to see me."

Rover stopped bouncing and sat at the door, looking at me with what might have been sarcasm on his furry face.

"Yeah, alright. It's been awhile. So what." I let him out before Grant stepped out of the car.

"Prepare to be accosted. Rover seems to think you're here to see him."

"Hey, buddy! Come here, you crazy dog. What's happening?" There was pandemonium, inside the car and out, while the guys exchanged greetings. I got my jacket and closed the hot pink door behind me.

"Hi," Grant finally said to me. "You look great."

"Thanks for noticing, but it's nothing special."

Pointing back to himself, he said, "Is this grubby enough for you? I packed light and didn't think to bring my sweatpants covered in paint stains."

He had on wrinkle-free black cargo pants (how is that done?), a black T-shirt, and a green down vest that matched his eyes. I tried to imagine him in stained sweats. Couldn't do it.

"Where are we going anyway?" he asked.

"I thought you might want to go to the beach first."

"I'm ready. Let's go." He held his door open for Rover to jump into the back seat, then got behind the wheel. "Same beach? Or somewhere new?"

It was refreshing to see that we weren't going to have the old, tired debate about whether he should open car doors for me. I got in the passenger side.

"Let's go to a different one. It's high tide and the jetty beach isn't safe. Just down from there is a more open place and I won't have to worry about you-know-who getting swept out to sea."

"You're not just taking me somewhere out of the way so we're not seen by any of your friends?" He grinned.

"No. I don't care who sees us, and I'll prove it to you," I said and smiled back. "Later."

After a moment he said, "You really do look great. I thought you said not to dress up. You look pretty fine to me."

I had on jeans, my Groucho Marx sweatshirt, and clean sneakers. Obviously this dude was easy to impress.

"That's only because you're not used to seeing me with my jumpsuit off."

Oops.

Grant grinned even bigger. "Whatever you say."

"Oh, shut up. You know what I meant."

The beach was unusually windless. Grant held my hand and we walked facing into the late sun. We'd gone over half a mile before we realized it.

"Hey, I know you're in shape for walking all day but I'm not," Grant said as he bent from the waist and stretched his hamstrings. "Want to go sit somewhere?"

We'd been talking about nothing in particular – his week at work, the Mariners, tourists, traveling. I have never had such a great walk.

"Oh, wow, I almost forgot." I held up his wrist and looked at his watch. "We've got to go." I turned back down the beach, pulling him along.

"Where're we going?"

"Pappy's. You said you wanted to sit. They've got bars-tools."

JESSICA WAS STILL behind the bar. The moment she set eager eyes on him, I started to doubt the wisdom of taking Grant to Happy Hour.

"Oh my god, Lainey! Please tell me this is your single cousin from out of town."

It went downhill from there. Good thing there weren't many customers because the few who wanted Jessica's attention had to bang an empty glass on the bar. Grant got a fresh coaster every time he picked up his beer. When Curly came in and Jessica got off duty, she immediately dragged me into the bathroom.

"Get a grip, Jess," I told her after she finally depleted her repertoire of porn movie sounds, her usual way of indicating that there was a hot guy in the vicinity. "I swear, if you don't stop embarrassing me..."

"What? Don't say it. You *will* let me be bridesmaid at your wedding. You *have* to. I'm your best friend!"

"I'm still taking bids. Would you please calm down? I'm trying to show Grant how a nice small town like Eden Beach really is. And you come off like a starving mountain lion eyeing a poodle."

"Sorry. Can I sit next to him? I promise not to drool."

I guess it could've been worse. At least Grant got to meet Twitch, who I consider the best Eden has to offer in the way of characters. The two of them chatted like old drinking buddies, and I was proud. Another plus was the absence of creepy caddies. There was only Spider and Tucson Johnny, and I knew that Johnny didn't care what guys I went out with, as long as I was happy. He was a lot like my mother that way. And due to Spider's preoccupation with whatever the voices inside his head were saying, I doubt whether he had ever noticed that I wasn't a dude.

Grant and I decided to finish our beers at the bar with Jess, then go get something to eat. "Sorry there isn't the usual action here today," I lied. "I wanted you to see more of the local color."

"What do you mean? I'm colorful," Jess said with a flounce of her magenta hairdo.

"Yes, you are," Grant said. "And I'm having fun, Lainey, so don't worry so much. This is a great place. Who exactly is Pappy, anyway?"

"I forget." Jess shrugged. "I think he's some dead guy."

I sighed. "Jessica isn't known for having an insatiable curiosity. Besides, she's only been living here all her life. Hey, I'm starving," I said quickly, because I couldn't remember who Pappy was either.

Grant said, "What about that place on the docks? Good fish and chips?"

"Yeah, if you don't mind the cold. There's only outside tables."

"But it's protected," Jess said. "I see people go there all the time, especially days like today. Go. It will be romantic." She batted her eyelashes.

"Good choice then. Thanks for the tip, Jessica. It's been a pleasure," he said as we got up. For a second I thought he was going to kiss her hand. Thankfully he just gave her his gorgeous smile and we left her to stew in her own juices, as it were.

We got our jackets out of the car, gave Rover a serious, "Stay!" and walked to the diner on the docks. It really was a beautiful evening. The harbor was calm, a few tourists strolled on the boardwalk, and two hearty souls were still throwing crab rings off the low dock. Grant was silent while we waited for our order.

"Why so quiet?"

"Oh, just listening to the gulls, the ocean, breathing the salt air." He sat with his hands laced together behind his head, gazing at the harbor.

"What's here that isn't in Seattle?"

"Everything. A wholeness."

For once, I waited instead of blurting out something stupid.

He faced me and laughed. "You know what I'm saying? I don't mean to get all *Zen* on you or anything. But for all the soul Seattle has, it's missing a heart. Sometimes I go all week and never stop to feel anything, to appreciate how I fit into the whole scheme of things."

"Grant, seriously. Do you truly think that the people you just saw at Pappy's stop to consider the whole scheme of things?"

"Why are you so hard on them, Lainey? Twitch, for example, is one hell of an impressive dude. Tell me that guy doesn't know where he fits into the scheme."

"Okay, maybe Twitch," I said, but I was thinking he probably wouldn't have a clue what a scheme was. "But maybe you're blowing this all out of proportion. You're on like a mini-vacation. Everything looks and feels different and terrific. Maybe it's just the same-ol'-same-ol' but you're enjoying it more because you're not home. And I guarantee that Jess, for one, does not know where she fits in."

"You're so mean to her. What's up with that? She's nice."

Our baskets of fish and chips came at that moment. Grant ordered another bottle of Beck's and I said I was good. We ate.

"This might be our first argument." I smiled at him over a fillet dripping with malt vinegar.

"I'm sorry. I shouldn't have called you out on things I know nothing about."

"Yes, you should. From now on, I give you permission to call me out, whether you know what you're talking about or not. So, our first argument ends, you're forgiven, and I'm ahead one to nothing."

We smiled at each other and relaxed.

"You are right that I razz Jess, but I'm not mean. We give each other a hard time in ways that, if anyone else said it, they would have to die. She is a true friend, and I love her. She understands. I'm sorry that it shocked you. I should've warned you."

He sat back. "Lainey, don't ever warn me."

BACK AT THE pink door, Rover and I were escorted to the porch. Grant turned me to him, embraced me, and we kissed. Long and slow. When we separated, it took me a moment to feel my feet on the step.

"I'm not going to even ask you whether I can come in," Grant said. "Instead, I will tell you that I had a wonderful time, and that I look forward to seeing you tomorrow." He bowed over my hand, touching it lightly with his lips, and then looked up at me. "Oh, there is just one thing I wanted to ask you."

"What?" I gazed dreamily into his mysterious green eyes.

"How much did Scott tip you?"

My shove nearly knocked him off the porch and he laughed as he caught himself.

"Ow! I was just joking. This doesn't count as an argument, does it?"

I licked my finger and chalked up a point in the air in front of him. "Two to nothing. Now go home, you bum."

CHAPTER 12

IF I'D KNOWN in my previous relationships with men what I know now, I would have to laugh in their faces – the inept dolts. Somebody should tell them. They're doing it all wrong.

To say that my next day and, more importantly, my night were incredible would be like saying Alice Cooper is a snappy dresser.

It started with the thrill I got from seeing Rocks's face when Larson called my name as a "request of the guest" before Rocks had an assignment. For two days in a row I aced him and it felt *great!* Then I spent the day watching the two cutest golfers in the resort enjoy a round on a course that can't be matched for its unique beauty. Hemlock Hollows is my favorite of the two courses. Sure, the Bluffs has more panoramic views of the ocean, but the Hollows has the nooks and crannies of a real woods that make you say, "Whoa, there's a golf course in here!"

Anyway, Grant and Scott had a blast, and I was there. I did my job, probably better than usual, but it just didn't feel like I was working. More like I was getting to tag along with the fun guys. It doesn't get any better than that.

And then it did.

Grant insisted on taking me and Scott to dinner at Rosaria's.

"You're not going to believe this place. Absolutely the best Italian, *real* Italian cooking, you've ever had," Grant told him.

"Do I need to carry a piece and sit facing the door?" Scott asked.

"No," I told him. "For crying out loud, this is Eden Beach, not Jersey."

"Yeah, Scott," Grant said with derision. "Here, you want to bring your deer rifle."

Scott was in, and I said I'd meet them at Rosaria's at 7:00. I spent the better part of the afternoon figuring out what to wear, how to deal with Rover, and second-guessing every decision I made. In the end Rover and I took a soul-cleansing walk around the neighborhood, me breathing a healthy dose of oxygen and Rover giving a healthy dose of shit to all animals who dared to come near. It was therapeutic for both of us, and I had a solution. I called Jessica.

The outfit choices were a mixture of what I had available that Grant hadn't seen yet, and what I could borrow from Jess. Like the true friend she is, she came over immediately, carrying an armful of "date-wear."

"Lain, you've got to go with the teal tube top. It looks fantastic with the denim mini. Trust me. It's hot," Jessica recommended with a serious nod of approval.

I looked at myself in the mirror. I had on the miniskirt, but I wasn't about to even come close to trying on the tube top. "I don't think so, Jess. And no to the mini. Can't I just wear pants? No self-respecting girl over twenty-one actually wears miniskirts, do they?"

"I do, but only when I go out of town. Okay, no mini for you, you party-pooper. But at least try these."

She held up a pair of white denim capris.

"White? I can't wear white."

"Just this once, Lainey. Try it. What's the worst that can happen?"

"Well, okay. But I'm only going to drink white wine or vodka. And I won't touch any food."

In the end, we agreed on the capris, a jade green V-neck with a lacy yoke that I'd found at the consignment store, and my best sandals. I added the pearl earrings my mother had given me, and Jess gave me a thumbs-up.

"Just right, Lain. You're chic."

Chic. That's me, alright.

Then I was off to be wined and dined, with Rover riding shotgun in case I needed him for backup. Inside Rosaria's Grant greeted me with a kiss on the cheek and Scott held my chair. Our server was Stephanie again and she flashed me a sly wink to let me know she was *very* impressed. Not only was I out with the same guy twice, I had *two* guys. I felt so confident that I ate bread drenched in olive oil, pasta with marinara sauce, and drank red wine without getting any on me.

The three of us shared equally in the conversation as well as the food. The dynamics were different than on the golf course; I was off duty. Scott and Grant talked about them-selves, not their game, and encouraged me to tell more about myself. I was interesting. I was clever. I was engaging. And I wasn't even drunk.

When Grant ordered a second bottle of wine to go with dessert, Scott said that he really should be getting back to the resort. He needed to call his wife before she went to bed. How sweet is that?

Grant's face expressed such disappointment at Scott's words that I said, "I can drive you back later, Grant, if you want to stay a while and have another glass of wine."

Scott picked right up on it. "Hey, yeah. Would you, Lainey? I really don't want to spoil the fun, but I'm kind of an old fogey and can't keep up with you kids."

"Scott," Grant said, "You're thirty-three. You can stay up past ten."

"I know, but..."

"I don't mind. Really," I said, trying not to sound nineteen.

So it was decided, and after a little haggling over who was going to be allowed to pay the bill (Grant won), Scott left us.

And that's when things really got interesting.

After drinking a bit of the second bottle, Grant and I got the great idea to take the rest of it back to my place. After all, we were finished eating, it was getting late and the restaurant wanted to close, and Rover was waiting in the Jeep. It made perfect sense.

My living room doesn't have a lot going for it. I don't even have a TV. But it does have a couch, and a great fish box /coffee table that can fit two pairs of feet as well as a bottle and two glasses. There is also a real turntable with stereo speakers and a bitchin' collection of blues albums.

What more could you ask for?

I AM NOT a girl who kisses and tells. But if I were... wow, the things I could tell!

No. Change that. Some things are better kept to oneself. Not in that Dear-Diary-locked-up-hidden-under-your-pillow kind of way, but in the way that takes cerebral muscle. My memories of that night are under my full control and I don't want to dilute them by putting them into mere words. Poor Jess, though. She may never forgive me.

Late Sunday morning I managed to get Grant back to their cabin in time for them to catch the afternoon flight to Seattle. My timing was perfect, because there were no employees around to see me drop him off, or to see Grant take me in his arms and lay a big honkin' kiss on me. Once we could get our hands off each other, our good-byes were short.

"I'll phone you when I get back to my condo."

"Promise?"

"I promise. Don't go anywhere?" he asked, looking intently, pleadingly, into my eyes.

"I won't. I'll be here," was all I could say.

I HAD FORGOTTEN the worst part about falling in love. It's not as if I've done it that many times before, and never like this, but you'd think I would've remembered. Here you are having this wonderful time with someone who fills your every desire, and the moment he's gone you feel your life is over. Death by heartache.

I sulked the rest of the day. Didn't call my mom and dad, didn't call Jess, didn't go out of the house. I could tell Rover was fed up. He can be as sensitive as the next dog, but I knew I'd reached his limit for cuddling and baby-talk when he hid from me behind the couch.

The evening phone call from Grant helped to ease my pain. He was adoringly sweet, telling me repeatedly how great I was, how he couldn't get his mind off me. We stopped short of actual phone sex, but it was delicious anyway.

Real life resumed, and I went about the rest of the week torturing everyone around me with annoying mood swings. Guys in the caddie shack, the ones who knew me well enough to go beyond mere glowering, told me to take a chill pill, and other suggestions not that polite. One morning when Tiny Sue caught me smiling uncontrollably, she stated the obvious.

"So, Lainey's gettin' some."

I sat down in the chair next to her, knowing that we'd be left alone. She had put up her force field to all, except me.

"Make that past tense. He's been gone four days and I think I'm going through withdrawal. Amazing what we put ourselves through, isn't it? At twenty-four I should know better."

Sue patted my back and gave a small laugh. "You'll make it. In another week, great sex will go back to being the urban myth you thought it was last week."

"I doubt it, Sue. This was phenomenal." I glazed over for a moment, then pulled myself together. "Have you ever had a long-term relationship? If you don't mind my asking."

"Well, if you define 'long-term' as more than three weeks and 'relationship' as not waking up alone in the morning, then yeah. Once. But I'm through with that crap. I've got enough drama in my life."

She turned away, pretending to check out what was on the TV behind us. I let it go. No sense debating the pros and cons of love with anyone who didn't have a Grant, and, oh yeah, that's only me.

"Speaking of drama, what's happening with your issues with Management?"

Sue glanced around the room, then leaned towards me. "Keep a secret?"

"Boy, can I! You've no idea how well I can keep a secret. What?"

"I'm leaving this shithole."

"GET OUT! Oops, sorry." My outburst came from my shock at hearing not only her statement but the way she said it. Tiny Sue meant business.

We both looked around, but no one was paying any attention.

"I made the decision three weeks ago. The crap they dish out..." She jutted her chin towards the office. "I can't take it anymore. As soon as I get the rent deposit back on my place, I'm out of here."

"Where are you gonna go?"

"Pebble Beach. The US Open is starting now, and there's a good chance of getting picked up by minor players for short term. And then I hope to catch a break and get hired by a pro for a tour."

I was stunned. Excited for her and totally pissed at the same time. How could she leave?

"Yikes, Sue, what am I gonna do without you? You'd leave me here all alone with these assholes?"

"You're a big girl, Lainey, and way tougher than them. Besides, I've been here almost three years, so it's not like I'm wussing out. I've gotten all I can get out of this small-time gig and I want to advance. There's been a couple of pros who come here in the off season. I looped for them and they told me I was good enough to make it if I was ready to live that life, and now I'm ready."

"It would be pretty cool, I guess." I was still trying to get a handle on this new development. "But when you get hired, how do you know it will be someone you can trust? How will you know he's for real?"

She laughed. "How do we ever know? How about your guy? How do you know he's for real?"

"Oh, I know. He's not like the rest, he's… hold on." I squinted sideways at her. "You're teasing me, right?"

"Yeah, sorry, but you're just way too easy. I know it's a gamble, but what isn't? Other caddies have done it, and some of them weren't as good as I am. And I'm no dummy. I'll check out any dude that wants to hire me and make sure there are no strings attached."

"When? How will you get to Palm Springs?"

"Drive. I've put some of my stuff in storage, and the rest I'll throw in my car and go. There are some places that caddies share during the tournament where I can stay, and when I get the tour job I'll sell my car and take just what I can fit into a suitcase. It's as easy as that."

She was talking about a whole new world. I knew about tour caddies, but I'd never thought about the kind of life they lived. Traveling for six to nine months out of the year, hopping from one town to the next, staying in cheap motels.

"I hope you find a rich, kind and generous pro."

She laughed. "Yeah, me too."

"What about here? When will you tell them?"

"Let 'em guess. I don't have to tell them a damn thing."

Larson walked in then, clipboard in hand, and shouted Sue's name along with three others. Sue got ready to go out. When she bent down to pick up her jacket, she looked me straight in the eyes. "You'll keep quiet about this, won't you?"

"I promise. I'm really happy for you, Sue."

"Thanks. And I'm happy for you too." She turned to go but then spun back. "Have fun, Lainey. Just be careful."

CHAPTER 13

WHETHER I WAS ready or not, the wretched sun kept coming up and going down. Somehow I managed to get myself to the resort and schlep bags for rich golfers day after day. With Sue gone and Grant too busy with his work to leave Seattle, the routine of drowning my sorrows with the rest of the lonely souls at Pappy's seemed like a reasonable thing to do. So I was surprised when I saw Gail's '67 Mustang parked in the lot one afternoon. This was out of whack – she was my beach friend, not a tavern friend. She once told me that she and Stewart had been bar hounds in their younger days, but they outgrew it.

Jessica was tending bar as usual. She'd given up on trying to snub me until I'd tell all about my night with Grant, and she was talking to me again. She joked that her imagination was probably better than the reality anyway, but I knew she understood.

"Rough day at the office?" she asked, setting my draft on the bar. I sat next to Gail, who was next to a young guy I'd never seen before. He was chatting with Twitch, who had his usual stool at the far end.

"I dunno. I forget. What day is it?"

"Thursday. Time to get ready for another big weekend."

"Oh goodie," I said. "Hi, Gail. It's nice to see you, but what are you doing in this cruddy place?"

"Cruddy? It's not so bad. It's nicer than the smoky old dive I used to hang out in," Gail replied.

Twitch nodded in agreement. "Yep. That was quite a place. Had spittoons and a rail under the bar, no barstools."

Gail laughed. "Not that bar, Twitch. That one was even before my time. I'm talking about the Tides Tavern."

The guy sitting next to Gail said, "Spittoons? You're kidding. Were women even allowed in bars way back then?"

"Hey, Travis, don't insult Twitch," Gail said. "Just because it was an ancient bar doesn't mean Twitch is."

"No, no, he's right. It was quite a while ago." Twitch took an imperceptible sip of his beer. "I'm older than I look."

That cracked us all up, because face it, Twitch looked a-hundred-and-ten.

"Lainey, meet my nephew, Travis." Gail leaned back and the guy next to her reached across and shook my hand. He was about my age, and had the look of a guy who did manual labor for a living. And by this I mean, nice. He had shaggy, brown hair that swept behind his ears, a well-trimmed beard and mustache, and he wore stylish, rimless glasses.

"Hi, Travis. Here visiting?"

"No, I'm here for good. Moved a week ago, from the Silverton area. I'm staying at Aunt Gail's for a bit while I get my business off the ground."

"Hey," Gail said. "That's a good line. You should put it in an ad. 'Travis Woods Landscaping – Help me get my business off the ground.'"

He shook his head in disapproval and drank some beer.

"A landscaping business sounds doable," I said. "I'd think that there's plenty of business here for landscapers. People that own those big properties on the bluff who are hardly ever here, there aren't enough mowing crews to go around."

"That's what I told him," Gail said. "Not to mention the new homes and remodels that need the whole works. Well, maybe construction has slowed down, but there are still places that need work."

Jessica rejoined us after waiting on a group at the pool tables. "That's the truth. I hate seeing all those empty places and the yards going to seed."

Travis spoke up. "I've just got to get the word out that a contract with me is better than letting the property lose value."

"Maybe Lainey can get you some good contacts from Screaming Bluffs," Jess said. "You know some rich locals from out there, don't you, Lainey?"

Gail explained, "Lainey works out at the golf resort as a caddie."

"A caddie. That's cool. How do you like it?" Travis asked.

"Not a good day to ask. But it's okay, I guess. And yeah, I can help spread the word for your business."

"That'd be really nice. I appreciate it."

"Lainey," Gail said suddenly, "I'm glad we ran into you because I wanted to invite you to our place for the Fourth of July. Jessica said she'd come, so if you don't already have plans you should come too. If your boyfriend's in town you can bring him along."

I gave Jess the evil eye, to which she responded, "I didn't tell her that much. Just that you were seeing this guy..."

Gail interrupted, "And I met him, remember? When you two were walking on the beach?"

"Oh, yeah. I guess I don't have to keep him a big secret, anyway. The party sounds great, thanks for asking me. Jess and I will both have to work that day. Will that be okay?"

"Sure, that's fine. We'll have the barbecue going, and people will be coming and going from early afternoon until the fireworks start. Most people like to come down here to the boat basin to watch them."

"Yeah," Jess said. "Wait till you see it, Travis. It's a circus down here."

"Sounds terrific," he said. "I'm just a small-town boy and I can't tell you how glad I am to be on the coast where you can do fireworks. Can't wait."

"Alright then. So we'll see you girls there. Rain or shine," Gail said as she got up. "Let's go, kid. We're due back at the ranch. Stewie's cooking tonight and he won't start until he sees we're gonna be there to eat. So long, Twitch. See you on the Fourth."

Travis gave us all a polite goodbye and they left.

"Cute guy, huh?" Jess said rather unenthusiastically.

"Yeah, cute. So how come you're not lusting after him?"

"It's not like I lust after all men, Lainey. Some aren't my type."

"You mean the ones with manners?"

She tried to dope-slap me but I was too quick for her. It was good to be friends again.

"HI, MOM," I said into my cell phone from the comfort of my front porch step. The eastern sky showed the beginnings of a clear night and the last-quarter moon hung over the coast range. Traffic on the highway was infrequent and the neighborhood was quiet. Rover perked his ears and nose up, expecting more excitement, but he was out of luck.

"Lainey, what are you doing phoning on a Thursday? Is everything alright?"

"Yes, everything is fine. It's just that I know it's going to be a busy weekend, and since Sunday is the Fourth, I might not get a chance to call. Missed calling you last Sunday, and I didn't want you to worry."

"You know I don't worry about you. It is good to hear from you though, to find out what you're doing. Tell me what's new."

"Oh, everything's pretty much the same. Except that I have a kinda boyfriend." I'd tried to put that as matter-of-factly as possible. I don't think it came out right.

"A kinda boyfriend. Is that somewhere between getting engaged and just met him last night?"

The laughter in her voice assured me that she made no judgment call either way.

"Well, I did meet him only a few weeks ago, but we've talked a lot since then. Remember the guy I told you about? The one who took me to the Italian restaurant?"

"The one you said you weren't going to be moving too quickly with?"

"Yeah, that one. I think we've gotten to know each other pretty well and we still like each other. That's saying something, isn't it?"

"It is. He sounds nice, but I don't remember all that you told me about him. What's this kinda boyfriend's name?"

"Grant. He's from Seattle and I met him when he was here on a golf weekend with some buddies. Which makes me a little nervous because there's this unwritten rule at the resort that we're not supposed to see guests socially. But it really started out innocently – I'd caddied for him twice and we got to talking, and he asked me to show him the town, and I took him to the beach, then we went to eat, and I don't think anyone from the resort saw us, and anyway it wasn't like I planned it…"

"Lainey, you're rambling. Besides, I don't care about all that or what the resort people think. Tell me what he's like. Does he have a good sense of humor?"

"What do you think? He likes *me*. And Mom, he's so nice, knows all the right things to say, how to be sweet. You know what I mean?"

"Yes, I do. He sounds pretty special. He sounds good for you. I'm really happy, Lainey." She was quiet a moment. "How are you going to handle this long-distance romance thing?"

"I don't know. It's so hard. I miss him, Mom. Grant's only been able to come back once, but we call each other every night. I'm hoping he can come this weekend. I'll call him right after we hang up and I'll find out."

"Good. Do that, and whatever he tells you, remember that things will fall into place. They always do."

The words I needed to hear. I don't care if it's wishful thinking or sentimental optimism, I like to hear the words.

"Thanks, Mom."

"And don't worry so much about those unwritten rules. They're meant to be bent. Isn't that what you've always told me?"

"Absolutely. Thanks for reminding me."

"Okay, call your Grant now."

"Okay, bye, Mom. And tell Dad hi."

"I will. Talk to you soon. Stay good, Lainey."

I speed-dialed Grant immediately, hoping Mom's good karma was still on the line. He answered before the first ring ended.

"Hey there, baby. What's shakin'?" he asked in a terrible Elvis impersonation.

"You're in a good mood."

"I'm in a great mood." Thankfully he gave up on the Elvis, but his voice hinted at a surprise to come. "Business is finished for the week, everything is in order, I have staff standing by in case of disasters at properties over the weekend – a-*n-n-d*..."

"What? Grant, stop teasing. And WHAT?"

"I'm driving to Eden tomorrow. And I thought that if you're going to be around, maybe I could drop by, hang out a while."

"Grant! Are you serious? Are you really coming?" I scared Rover with my excitement and he came over to stare at me.

"Yes, really."

Calming down I said, "You're driving all the way down? Do you even have a car?"

"Yes, I even have a car. You think I only drive rentals? I happen to have a BMW that I've had since college. And although it's seen better days, it will make the trip easily."

"Are you coming by yourself?"

"By myself. No business partners, no golfing buddies, just me. Do you think you can stand a weekend with just me, or should I find something else to do?"

"I think I can handle it. How soon can you get here?"

My mind was not putting it all together yet. My body was doing all the thinking.

"I'll get an early start, should get there in early afternoon. You'll probably still be out at the golf course."

"Are you staying there?" There was probably a tiny whine in my voice. I couldn't help it.

"Well, here's the thing. Staying at the Bluffs would really put a dent in my finances – I mean I can afford to, if I have to. I'm not rich or anything, by their standards. That's why I'm driving down, not flying. But it's just that I'd rather spend what I have on..."

"Wait. Listen. You could stay here. With me. Is that an unheard of possibility?"

"If you're really sure, Lainey. I want to, but I know it's kind of early, you know, to be spending nights together. At least that's what people are telling me."

"What people? Are you talking about me to your friends?"

"Well, uh, yeah. But only really good friends. Lainey, I've been out of this relationship thing for so long, I don't know what I'm supposed to do."

His helplessness was giving me the boldness needed if we were ever going to get this thing off the ground.

"Look, I'm okay with it. Very okay. If you can stand this wreck of a house and a double bed instead of the fancy suite with a king bed you can get at the Bluffs, I want you to stay here."

"That's an easy choice to make. Your bed sounds better than anything I could dream of."

So it was settled. We both realized the enormity of the step we'd just taken. With that brief exchange, we had committed. I was breaking from my past, a past of impulsive hook-ups just because I was lonely. A past of hanging on to unresponsive guys while I waited for them to realize we were meant for each other. I now had a boyfriend. An honest-to-god boyfriend.

Grant said he'd be able to stay until Monday, but then he had to get back for work. That gave us most of four days, and three ecstatically long nights. He told me he could afford a round of golf on Saturday, if I'd caddie for him. I thought about it, but replied that it would be better if he played solo and I took whatever assignment came up. That way, our getting together would be totally clear of the *verboten*. Not to satisfy management's rules, which I'd taken my mother's advice to ignore, but my own. My rules were not only unwritten, they were inexplicable. Grant understood, and that's all that mattered.

We made plans to meet at my house on Friday (hidden key behind the mossy shingle on the east side of the house, if he got there before I did), but nothing else. My mind raced with the possibilities.

CHAPTER 14

GRANT AND ROVER were playing keep-away with a stick in the front yard when I got there. I was later than I wanted to be because my loop had taken forever. I hadn't even taken the time to wash the grime off my face or brush my hair, but Grant didn't seem to mind. He enveloped me in his big strong arms and kissed me within an inch of my life. We didn't speak for several minutes – just stood there making out in my front yard. It was crazy fun.

When we finally made it into the house, I insisted on a shower while Grant made himself at home. I had stayed up late cleaning the house and had gone to the store, so everything was in good shape and I could relax and enjoy. Grant noticed.

"You look great," he said when I came into the living room. This was due to the fact that I'd put on a robe when I got out of the shower, and my hair was wrapped up in a towel.

He had been sitting on the couch, sharing some cold cuts with Rover, but quickly got up and embraced me again. With my arms pinned, I could still reach the top of his pants and manage to undo them. He was halfway undressed before we hit the bed.

"Wait. I think it's my job to, uh... put the club cover on," I said, breaking away quickly to open the nightstand drawer.

"Lainey, you have a remarkable way with words."

"Wait till you see how remarkable I can be with club covers."

IT'S FUNNY THAT no one ever told me great sex could make your body go numb. I would've thought it worthy of at least one article in the *Cosmo* magazines I used to read. I wondered about this breach in every girl's right to know as I sat on the bench outside the caddie shack Saturday morning. My nerve endings were still tingling, so I almost missed the vibration of my cell phone that signaled an incoming text. Grant, having driven his own car to the Bluffs, was checking in at the pro shop as a single. His text read, "Waiting 4 u bluffs or hollows?"

Since I hadn't gotten an assignment yet, he was too early. We wanted to be on the same course, if not within eyesight of each other, so I anguished over my next move. Besides my clumsiness with texting (who did I ever have to text with?) it was policy, one that was frequently violated by caddies much swifter than I, that we not use cell phones on the course. I had to get this right before I got out there.

"stallll"

That was pretty close.

"Tidwell!"

I heard Larson's call from across the room and through the background TV noise.

"Rocks! Head out to the Bluffs."

I managed to poke more buttons and send another text before jamming the phone back in my pocket.

"g02blufs"

When I got off the shuttle, I saw Grant as I passed the pro shop. I smiled, relieved to see that he'd deciphered my message. He smiled back and winked, which made me giggle, which made Rocks turn around to look back at me. Why Rocks, today of all days?

"Ah. You likey?" He wiggled his butt. "I knew you couldn't resist."

I almost gagged. "Oh, please. I was just thinking of something funny. Nothing to do with you."

"Sure, sure, Sweetcheeks. Just say the word and I'll let you get a closer look at this fine ass."

He wiggled it again for me, I suppose as an enticement. I was determined not to show my revulsion.

"Rocks. We have to work together. It's going to be a long day. Please don't make it worse."

He leered but said nothing, and we went to meet our guests. Rocks and I had one each of a foursome, with two players carrying their own bags. My Mr. Tiller was an average weekend player, he told me, and wouldn't mind if I helped him pick the right club. I knew he was sizing me up, and I don't mean just as a caddie. There were all the usual jokes about my height, and his eyes were locked on my boobs. I was not going to let it spoil my day. I could afford to lose this turkey.

"Ahem. Careful, Mr. Tiller," I said with a smile when he finally lifted his eyes. "Just so you know, sometimes I've been known to accidently drop clubs off the bluff when I get flustered."

"Whoa there, sister. No need to get flustered. I'm sorry if I offended you."

"No problem, Mr. Tiller. I know you want to have a terrific round today, and I'll try to make sure that you do."

He eyed me suspiciously. Good. That's the attitude I wanted to see.

When all four had teed off, I sneaked a peek at my cell phone while Tiller walked ahead.

"Right behind u"

I turned to see Grant and three other men waiting at the starter's curtain. He had been matched up with a threesome, common practice on a busy course. With any luck, we'd be able to spot each other from time to time, and would finish our loops minutes apart.

It soon became evident that the two sets of golfers weren't in the same league. Our foursome scattered in different directions on the fairways as if they'd been blown by the wind, nobody really knowing how to play the course. Grant's group played better and was having to wait at every tee box. This meant that by No. 5, they were putting while our players had barely finished teeing off No. 6, and I could sneak a glimpse of Grant on the green. He was having fun, kidding around with the other guys. All four looked athletic and dressed like they had money and good taste, a combination I didn't see often around here. None of them needed a caddie.

"What hole are you playing, Tidwell?" Rocks asked. "Something more interesting on 5?"

I hadn't noticed that he'd been hanging back behind me and now moved alongside.

"Don't worry about it, Rocks. You carry your bag and I'll carry mine. I don't hear Mr. Tiller complaining."

The fact was, Tiller had been asking for my advice on every stroke. I had the sick feeling he would've liked it even better if I wore high-heeled boots, carried a whip, and hurled abuse at him.

"You chicks have it so easy," Rocks said. "All you gotta do is smile pretty and you get these dopes eating out of your hands."

His whining attitude made me think of one of my dad's favorite comments. "Rocks, the glory of life is not in winning, but in playing a poor hand damn well."

The lesson was lost on him. He watched Grant's foursome, then showed me his evil smile again.

"I don't think you can pull it off, Tidwell. You might be trolling for those studs, but you're stuck with Tiller here and there's not enough of you to go around."

"You know what?" I shot at him over my shoulder. "You're really starting to annoy me. Why don't you catch up with your guest and maybe we can move this game along? We're holding up the pace of play."

"Shit. Those boys' club cocksuckers can kiss my ass," he said under his breath and quickened his step. Rocks talked tough, but he knew better than to let the marshals see him dragging behind his player.

I waited for Tiller, the farthest back of the four, and handed him a 4-iron when he walked up to his ball. "Go long and low, straight at that fir tree in the distance, and you'll be in good shape, Mr. Tiller."

"Can do, darlin'. Right on the ol' sweet spot." He ratcheted over his ball like a rusty lawn chair for a full minute, then topped it for a 50-yard worm-burner.

"Not that low, Mr. Tiller." I smiled, sighed, and hoofed ahead. I was thinking that a whip would come in handy.

At the turn, one of our players caught on that the group behind was riding up our butts so he convinced Tiller and pals to get a drink and let the others play through. I waited off to the side of the #10 tee box, pretending great interest in all four of the hotshots. Grant came out of the port-a-potty and had to walk right past me. That was because I happened to be standing next to his bag.

"Hey, cutie," he whispered.

"Hey, yourself. This is the pits. I wish I was bagging for one of you guys."

"Me too." He brushed close, so close I felt a flush of heat. It was a nice heat.

"Yikes. That's not helping, you know."

He gave a soft laugh and picked up his bag. "Hope I run into you again sometime, caddie."

I was feeling much better. That was until I turned and saw Rocks staring at me with that evil grin. This wasn't good. I braced myself for an onslaught of disgusting insults. But he stayed where he was. I kept my eye on him as our foursome came out of the snack bar, and his player handed him an airline-size bottle of Jack Daniels. Rocks gave a nod of thanks,

138

opened it, drank some and pocketed the illicit bottle. Then he must have told a stupid joke at my expense, because all five of them turned in my direction and snickered.

God, I hate men.

The back nine was even slower, as Tiller's game went to hell. When his strokes went into double-digits on three consecutive holes because he couldn't take his eyes off me, I finally had to ask him to stop.

"You're wasting the whole experience, Mr. Tiller. You're not even trying. Why don't you pay more attention to your swing and forget I'm here?"

"Ah, come on, darlin'. That other caddie said you'd be extra nice to me if I was nice to you." He winked. "I give you a sizable gratuity and then later..."

"What! He said what? That asshole! That dirty, lying, perverted dickhead!" I scanned the fairway to find Rocks and saw that he was eighty yards away, upwind, and hadn't heard me. Maybe I had time to cool off before I brained him with Mr. Tiller's driver.

Tiller sputtered, losing what little civility he'd thought he had. "Now, now, I don't mean to upset you. Are you allowed to yell like that while you're working?"

"Upset?" I yelled louder into his stricken face. "Do I seem upset? Why would I possibly be upset? Could it be because, here you are at a top-class golf course, and you blow your whole game today because you think you're hiring a hooker instead of a caddie? Could I be upset because that sorry sack of shit over there turns caddying, this honorable, decent profession, into something ugly by pandering to clueless horndogs? WHY would THAT upset me?"

Maybe that was over the top. I could see that Tiller was so shaken by now that he probably hadn't heard the insult. I took a deep breath.

"It's alright. I'm calm. It was just a little misunderstanding." I picked up the club he'd dropped, wiped it clean, and gently placed it in the bag. I picked up the bag and smiled sweetly. "Let's hurry, Mr. Tiller. We don't want the marshal to notice we're lagging behind, do we?"

He followed me in silence and stayed that way for the rest of the game. So did the other players. No one, not even Rocks, called me out on my supreme meltdown.

Huh. Who knew it would be that easy? I think Tiny Sue would be proud.

GRANT'S BMW PULLED out of the main parking lot as I passed, and he followed me home. When we were sitting together on the couch and I'd had a few well-earned swigs of beer, I told him the story. His first reaction was a furrowed brow, skinny eyes, and a set jaw. Then the corners of his mouth slowly went up and his lovely crinkles returned.

"Man, am I sorry I missed that! You must have been dynamite."

"That's what you've got to say? Aren't you going to go beat up Rocks for me? Defend my honor?"

"What, and spoil all your fun?" He threw his arm around me and pulled me into him. "No, Lainey. He's all yours. I have a feeling the payback he gets from you will be worse than anything I could do."

Grant had me describe the scene again. I had to admit it sounded pretty funny, and I cheered up. After hot showers and cold beers, we talked about other things, including where we'd go for dinner.

"Can we go to Rosaria's again, or are you tired of it?" he asked.

"No, I'm not tired of it. I haven't tried everything on the menu yet."

CHAPTER 15

THE RESORT WAS packed Sunday. Didn't these people have somewhere else to go on the Fourth of July? Watch the downtown parade? Stand in line at the city park an hour for a hamburger? Set off illegal fireworks at the beach and catch the driftwood on fire? Judging by the parking lots already overflowing with SUVs when I got there, golf is evidently the new American pastime.

Larson had me scheduled to loop Hemlock Hollows before I'd walked in the door. I was relieved when I saw that I'd be working with Tucson Johnny and Jug Ears. No sign of Rocks. The bad news was my assigned guest turned out to be as big a creep as Mr. Tiller and a worse golfer. This guy was a combination of stupid, crass, and macho rolled up into one big ugly jock. I mean really – a neon-yellow sweater and fleece cargo pants? And to top it off, I think he was bipolar because he'd switch from a club-throwing temper tantrum to a raunchy comedy act in seconds. I kept looking over my shoulder to see if Rocks was hiding somewhere in the dunes laughing his head off.

At least Jug Ears and Johnny were around to bolster my spirit. Jug Ears even remarked that this dude's jokes were terrible. "If I ever get that bad, Lainey, would you just smack me?"

"Count on it."

Tucson Johnny added, "Just think. Somewhere in Eden right now there's a nice little family having a great, touristy day, because their jerkwad of a dad is out here with us. Sorry you drew him, Lainey. I'da switched if I had seen it comin'."

"Yeah," Ears said, "me too."

"Thanks, guys. But I'll make it," thinking again of my dad's saying. Although it didn't seem fair that I was dealt a poor hand two days in a row.

To tune out the jerkwad, I daydreamed of what Grant might be doing in town. He'd decided to spend the day wandering around and "getting to know" the people. I told him there would be more out-of-towners here than locals because of the Fourth, and he said that would make it entertaining. I pictured him walking around the crowded shops and sidewalks, cute and sexy in his chambray shirt and perfectly pressed chinos. I hadn't had the heart to tell him that he wouldn't blend in very well, with tourists or locals.

If I weren't so stubborn, I could have gone with him. But no, I had to insist on working to show my independence, my integrity and dedication. What a bunch of crap. If I'd known I was going to bag for Bozo Superjock I would've faked an illness. Instead, I was here getting sicker by the moment.

I peeked at my cell phone. No messages, and it was 2:30. I found myself "counting holes," the habit bag-packers have of pushing to the 18th, usually so they could get assigned another bag. We were on the 16th fairway; I could last another half hour or so.

"Lainey, you going to hang around, get another loop in?" Johnny asked as we followed the players off the tee box.

"Hell no. I've had it. Besides, I've got a party to go to."

"Cool. Yeah, I think I'll scoot, myself. Where's your party, if you don't mind my asking?"

"You know Gail and Stewart? They live south of town?"

"No kidding! Yeah, I know them. That's the party I was thinking of going to!"

"I'll see you there then. Should be a nice, relaxing way to end this sucky day."

"I'd say you deserve it, Lainey. Let's do it."

I called Grant as soon as I got to my car. He said he was on the boardwalk and ready to head back to the house. He'd meet me there. He didn't sound all that chipper, but then I wasn't exactly perky either.

Once we were together and I'd gotten into some clean clothes, the three of us got into his car (I'd had direct orders from Gail to bring Rover). When asked how he enjoyed his day, Grant told me it was "alright."

"Did you get bored?"

"No. Not bored. I don't know. It just felt weird." He drove without saying anything, following my directions to Gail's farm. "How long do you want to stay at this party?"

"Until nine or so. Then we'll come find a place to park to watch the fireworks at the boat basin. Why?"

"I don't know. I feel kind of stupid, not knowing anyone."

"It will be fine. These are very casual, friendly people. I'm sure you'll like them and they'll like you. If you're not having a good time, we'll leave early."

"No, I don't want you to have to leave on my account."

"We'll see, okay?"

Gail's place was an old farmhouse, set back from the road and protected from the wind by a line of fir trees. In a shaded part of the big yard, Stewart was manning the grill and there were several dishes of salads and picnic foods spread on long tables.

"Lainey!" Stewart greeted me in his always cheerful way. "Glad you could make it. Pour yourself a cold one. I think Gail went inside for something, but she'll be here in a minute." He switched the spatula from his right hand and reached to shake Grant's. "Howdy. I'm Stewart. Happy to meet you."

"Hi, Stewart. I'm Grant. Thanks for letting Lainey bring me along. This is a great place you have here."

"Oh, yeah. But it's way too much work for us. One of these days, I'll be looking for a nice little place in town, maybe with a postage stamp yard and rocks instead of lawn."

Gail came towards us and greeted Rover, letting him jump on her until he spotted Angel and the two of them sped off to run circles around the other partiers.

"Hi, Grant. Nice to see you again. Glad you could join us. And don't let this guy bullshit you. He loves this place. If he'd just quit starting projects that don't need doing, he could relax and enjoy it more."

"It's not me," Stewart said. "It's that nephew of yours. He's the one that's been going crazy with the projects. He's a slave driver."

"Yeah, he's a worker alright," Gail said as she directed our attention across the yard towards Travis. He was sitting on the grass with a girl I knew from Pappy's, and from the looks of things, it was hard to tell who was working who.

"So, Grant," Gail continued, "I hear you're from Seattle."

They talked, I drank some beer, and things fell into place. We walked around a bit, found Twitch, Tucson Johnny, and Jessica, and I introduced Grant to a couple other friends. We filled paper plates with huge amounts of food and found a cozy spot under a tree.

"See? It's not so bad," I said with my mouth full of the most delicious steak I'd ever tasted. That Stewart was a master at the grill.

"I don't know what's bothering me." Grant's voice sounded too serious for a picnic. He put down his plate and looked around the yard as if trying to find someone. "This is really like something out of a movie. It's so… wholesome."

"Yikes. Wholesome? No one wants that."

"No. That's not the right word."

I let him struggle to get his thoughts together while I tried to guess what the yummy concoction of pasta-and-green-stuff was that I was eating.

"In Seattle," he went on, "there's structure, a known distribution of space. It's gigantic, I know, but it's structured in very simple terms. Terms I understand. Here, where there's not nearly as much diversity and it should be simple, I can't get focused. Things are too… fuzzy."

He said this with such fervor that I had to stop eating.

"What do you mean? What's fuzzy? Life is very clear here – we eat, drink, sleep, work, and if we're lucky, sometimes we screw. Don't they do that in Seattle? Oops, I forgot. That last one not so much."

His smile returned. "Funny. Keep it up and we'll see who gets lucky or not."

I was glad to see his humor back, but something was definitely bothering him. I pursued.

"This small-town life isn't for everyone, I'll admit. But it kinda grows on you. Don't you think?"

"Maybe. Walking around town today started out fun. I was people-watching, enjoying the holiday atmosphere. Then it occurred to me that they all looked pretty much the same. The snatches of conversations I overheard sounded the same. Don't you ever get tired of the sameness?"

"No. Not at all." I really hoped he wasn't going there. "Are you saying I'm boring?"

"No! Not you, Lainey. I don't mean anything like that."

"Good. Now shut up and eat, and I'll tell you about *my* day."

My storytelling talent saved the day again, and soon he was laughing at my description of the Hacker from Hell. The next time I have to suffer another loop like that, I'll try to remind myself that it will seem funny later.

Grant got more sociable as we moved around, talking to my friends and enjoying the party. We did our part in helping to finish off the keg of beer and things started winding down. It was time to go watch the fireworks.

Gail and Stewart made a point of checking out the sobriety of everyone getting behind the wheel, and in some cases designated another driver. I greatly appreciated that Grant passed the test. I rounded up Rover and we drove back to town.

The boat basin was already in full swing with families crowding the parking lots and boardwalk. There were blanketed folks huddled in lawn chairs and drinking from thermoses, and T-shirted kids running amok with bags of store-bought fireworks and butane lighters. There wasn't enough wind to carry the smoke away and a stinky haze hung over the pavement where kids were scattering unwary pedestrians and dogs with those lit, spinning, buzzing things.

"How come Rover doesn't freak out with the noise and stuff?" Grant asked. We were walking arm in arm, me with Rover on the leash.

"I don't know. He seems to like it. I think he's just always up for a party."

We skirted the area that had the biggest bunch of dangerous pyromaniacs, and steered towards the better-supervised kids with responsible adults.

"How about you?" I asked. "Are you freaking out with all this fuzziness?"

"Nah, I'm okay. Add a few pot-smokers and meth freaks and it reminds me of Pioneer Square on a Saturday night."

"Really? I'd like to see that."

"That could be arranged."

He was about to kiss me when a bang sounded from the other side of the river. The first of the city-orchestrated fireworks burst into a red, white, and blue fountain across the sky. Oohs and aahs came from the crowd and we all marveled until the fire department's stockpile ran out. It lasted about forty-five minutes and received rave reviews. Even Grant had to admit it was "pretty good for a small town."

As we mingled with the departing families, we bumped into Travis and the girl we'd seen him with earlier.

"Hey, guys!" he said, pretty drunkenly. "Wasn't that the coolest? Wow."

"Yeah, it was awesome," the girl said. She was having trouble focusing.

"Yes, very impressive," Grant said. He put his arm around me and pulled me close, maybe to protect me from getting bumped by other passing drunks.

"Well, have a nice night," Travis said with a grin, and we went our separate ways.

I was starting to realize that we were all pretty wasted. Thank goodness we only had to drive a few blocks on back streets and we made it home without mishap. I won't say that we were passing-out drunk, but sex was out of the question. Our exhausted bodies and blurred brains were not exactly in a romantic mood.

At 6:45 the radio on my nightstand blasted us awake with George Thorogood's "Bad to the Bone."

"Jesus," I croaked.

"That's a bit much," Grant said as he hit the OFF button.

We stumbled around in an embarrassed silence as we got dressed and Grant got his things together.

"Do you want coffee? Or anything?" was all I could think of to say.

"No thanks. I'll get it on the road." He gave me a sad smile and I fell against his chest.

"I don't want you to go. And I don't want to go to work today." I was close to tears. "I want… I want… I don't know what I want."

He hugged me and said softly, "Lainey, I have to go, and you have to go to work."

"But my work sucks. I hate those asshole golfers, and those asshole caddies, and everything."

"You know they're not all assholes. Lainey," he pushed me back and looked into my face, "you're a good caddie. You're what keeps golfers coming back. And anyone who's worth a shit can see that you love it."

"No I don't. I hate it."

He laughed. "You can hate it for a few more minutes, then you're going to get out there and get a bag. You'll get a savvy golfer who respects the game and respects the help of a good caddie."

I wiped my face on his shirt and sighed. "Okay, Boss. I can do it if you say so." I sniffed. "I'll be thinking about you, up there in your structured, unwholesomeness of high-rises and meth freaks."

"Do." He held me tight again, then gave me a long, sweet kiss. "Bye, Lainey. I'll call you tonight."

I stood in the doorway and watched him go to his car. He turned before he got in and said, "I really did have fun. Thank you."

"Anytime, fella."

CHAPTER 16

HE WAS RIGHT. I had the best day that I've had so far, except for when I caddied for him, of course. Coming in as late as I did meant a smaller pool to draw from, and when a late-starting woman golfer asked for a female caddie, I was the only one there. She was the first woman I'd ever bagged for and I was duly impressed. Because she had the perfect mix of serious golf and casual attitude, the loop was easy and fun. We talked about her potential to make the cut in the LPGA, and about competition in general. She was interested in my work as a caddie, having never tried it herself. Sometime during the loop I felt the thrill return, the excitement of knowing I was right where I should be, doing what was right for me.

Before going to Pappy's I swung by the post office to pick up my usual collection of junk mail. Mixed in with several days' worth of advertisements and sweepstakes offers was a nice surprise – a postcard from Tiny Sue. The photo was a shot of a bunker overlooking a rocky shore, mountains visible beyond a tranquil cove.

Sue's crammed message on the back read, "There's something wrong with the ocean here. As you can see, it's too flat. I miss Eden's ocean, & its weather, & SOME of the people, like you. I'm having fun, working hard, & REALLY loving the class of golfers AND caddies here. Started working for pro-ams, & now a Srs. player's hired me for the Champions tourney in WA at end of July & Sun River in August. Want to meet up? Sue".

The fact that she was thinking about me made me tear up. Considering my great day on the course and now this, my sisterhood sensitivities were working overtime. What the hell – I might as well keep the vibe alive and go see how Jess was doing.

Pappy's had its usual post-holiday Monday afternoon crowd, which came close to sapping every bit of joy right out of me. One look at Jessica's half-sunburned face and magenta-punk hairdo saved me.

"Yikes, Jess. You've got raccoon eyes like caddies get."

"Nice, huh? I wore my shades all day yesterday and forgot to sunscreen. My face hurts like hell."

Travis had come from the pool table and joined me at the bar.

"It should, because it's killing us," he said with a smile.

"Bite me, Four-eyes. Some of us have to work indoors and don't get to see the sun as often as you tree-huggers do."

Obviously, these two had gotten past the polite conversation stage of budding friendships. I guessed I'd better join in if I wanted to catch up.

"So, Travis, are you having a thing with that girl? The one from the party?"

Jess smiled. "You mean Mattress Marta. Yeah, where is she, Travis? Too early in the day for her to come out of her cave?"

Travis hung his head in halfhearted embarrassment and came up with a grin. "Oh come on, give me a break. It's only the first time I've partied with anyone here."

"And you had to pick the town skank," Jess went on. "Nice move."

I took pity on Travis and gave Jess a shot. "Like your reputation is so spotless?"

"She's got you there, Jess," Twitch piped up from his end of the bar.

"Hey, who asked you?" Jess said, barely missing him with a bar towel.

Travis challenged me to a game of pool while we waited for Jess to finish her shift. Afterwards the three of us decided to get a pizza and go to Jess's to watch a movie. I knew I'd be getting a call from Grant, but was glad to have friends keep me occupied meanwhile.

"Okay if I ride with you, Lainey? It's better to leave my truck here in public parking than in Jess's apartment complex. No offense, Jess."

"None taken. All that lawn care equipment wouldn't stand a chance in my neighborhood."

"Sure, Travis. I'll bring you back on my way home," I said. "We'll pick up the pizza, Jess, and meet you at your place."

Rover was elated when he saw Travis get into the Jeep. My dog has an excellent memory for good guys. He will totally snub Rocks and his crew if they walk past him, but wag like crazy if he sees Jake or Tucson Johnny a block away. Smart dog.

I asked Travis, "So, how's your business doing? You get many clients lined up yet?"

"Plenty. I love small towns – one or two people get to know you and your reputation spreads like wildfire."

That made me think of Mattress Marta and, judging by his reddening face, his mind must have gone the same direction. My laughter made him laugh, and that was how the whole evening went. Once we'd added Jess and a Chris Rock movie to the mix, we got downright goofy.

When my cell phone buzzed, Jess put the movie on pause. "Tell your boyfriend you still think he's hot and to make it quick 'cuz we're watching a movie."

I stepped outside and was giggling when I said, "Hi."

"Wow, you sound quite a bit happier than when I left you this morning," Grant said.

"I'm over at Jess's." I held the phone to my chest and yelled back inside for them to continue watching without me. "Sorry about that. So, how are things in the big city? Do you miss me yet?"

"I've been missing you all day. It's hard to keep my mind on work, but life goes on." He sighed, sounding truly miserable. "July is really busy for me, because the tourists come to town and they see something they like, consider living here or starting a business. Most of them are just tire-kickers, but I still have to show them properties."

His mood seemed to lighten as he talked more about his work. I was glad he was sharing his life with me, and his stories had me imagining what it would be like if I were there. When he began winding down, I told him about caddying for the savvy LPGA hopeful.

154

"Man, that's just what I wanted to hear. You had a good loop, now you're hanging with good friends. I knew you'd pull through, Wild Thing."

"Wild Thing? That's what you're calling me?"

"Yeah," he said with defiance. "It suits you. Don't you like it?"

"I don't know. Could be worse, I guess. But, Grant... hey, I'm gonna have to come up with a pet name for you now."

"No you don't. Grant is fine."

"Grant," I said, choking up just a little, "it's not all good. You're not here. I miss you." The tears started. I stopped talking so that he wouldn't be able to tell.

"I miss you too. But we'll see each other again soon. I don't know when, but we'll figure something out." Then with a pretense of toughness, he said, "We can make it, because we are strong of character and pure of heart."

"Are you drunk?"

"No. Are you?"

"A little. But I'm still not as crazy as you."

"Are too."

Life was good again.

ROCKS HAD MANAGED to steer clear of me for days, whether deliberately or by coincidence I couldn't tell. Chicken-shit does match his personality type, so I guess he knows I'm out to get him for telling Mr. Tiller that I offered more than caddie services. By not getting in Rocks's face right away, I would have time to cool off and plan a colder, better revenge. He deserved more than a hysterical, raging tirade in the caddie shack. He deserved a long, slow death.

I was going to need Jessica.

While I waited for her to join me on my side of the bar at Friday's happy hour, Travis came in and took the barstool next to me. I was glad to see him. His sense of humor and directness fit so well with ours, it was easy for us to become fast friends.

"Hey, Kemo Sabe," he said. "Long time, no see."

"Kemo Sabe – that's a good one. Can I borrow it? I'm looking for a nickname for someone."

"Feel free."

Jess came over to wait on him and greeted him with, "Hi, hippie."

"You can have that one too, Lainey, if you want. But it's kinda worn out."

"No, thanks. That won't work."

Jess got him his beer and we gave each other the mini versions of our workweek.

"So what's up for tonight?" he asked. "You guys got anything planned?"

"Lain wants me to help her plan a bitch of a payback for a caddie who dissed her."

I grunted. "That's putting it mildly."

Travis asked, "Who's the caddie?"

"Rocks," Jess said. "You know him?"

"I'm not sure. Is he one of those guys I've seen skulking in the back of the parking lot waiting for his dope dealer?"

Jess's eyes met mine. We shared a simultaneous inspiration of nastiness.

156

"He is now," I said.

Our strategy was to let Rocks's own paranoia work against him. All we had to do was plant a seed here and there, and stand back to watch.

Jess said, "The next time I see Spider, or Twila, or one of those other tweakers, I'll let them overhear me say I saw Rocks hanging out back there. I could say to Curly, "I wonder what he's doing," and Curly will undoubtedly tell me that that's the usual place to make a score. He loves to brag about how he knows everything that goes on around here."

"And I think I can pull Tucson Johnny in to start the rumor at the caddie shack," I said. "That way Rocks won't know I had anything to do with it. Until I want him to, that is."

"So, let me get this straight," Travis said as he set his beer on the bar. "You spread the word he's trying to score some dope of some kind, and the dealers will come looking for him."

"Yeah," Jess said, "dealers do their best business with the caddies. We all know that."

"Does this guy even use? Oh wait. I guess with a name like 'Rocks' it stands to reason."

I frowned at him. Jess explained, "He means crack. You know, *rocks*?"

"I know what he means," I fibbed. "No, not that kind. He named himself Rocks because it's a golf term. A cute word for golf balls."

"I know that," Travis said.

"Anyway, I don't think he uses any hard stuff. But I've seen him at the caddies' parking lot buying prescription pain meds. A lot of the guys use them if they do a lot of dub-dubs."

"What are dub-dubs?" Travis asked.

"That's what they call it when they carry two bags for two loops in a day."

"Okay, I didn't know that. So, tell me how this hurts him. Once he tells the dealer he's not in the market, it's over, isn't it?"

Jess smiled. "Not when dealer number one hears that Rocks bought from dealer number two at a higher price."

I continued the explanation. "And dealer number two hears he's paying big money to dealer number one. They'll both think he's an easy target and follow him around trying to sucker him into buying their product."

Travis said, "Do you women know what you're doing, messing around with turf wars? I mean, dealers are dangerous dudes. You don't want to really hurt this guy, do you?"

"They won't hurt him," Jess said. "Drug dealers around here aren't like in the city. They're basically stupid townies who can't get a job, and harmless to anyone who's not buying. They'll probably just hassle him for a couple of days, then they'll forget why and leave him alone."

"And meanwhile," I said, "Rocks will go crazy trying to disassociate from the hard-core druggies."

"Yeah," Jess continued with a phony compassion. "You know how much he prides himself as a Super Stud. Won't it be a shame when word gets out? Everyone knows dopers are worthless in bed."

I smiled. "Isn't it terrible what false stories about a person can do?"

Travis looked at me, then at Jess, and said, "Remind me never to piss you two off."

158

CHAPTER 17

WHEN I TOLD Grant how Jess and I were going to get even with Rocks, he had much the same reaction as Travis.

"Jeez, Lainey. That's kind of harsh. Spreading rumors that a guy is in the market for dope could really do some damage."

"I don't know what the big deal is. How is making him out as a doper any worse than him making me out as a hooker?"

He didn't have an answer, so we changed the subject. As part of our regular nighty-night phone conversations since he'd returned to Seattle, we shared our daily moments that had seemed monumental at the time – things we wouldn't tell anyone else who would, understandably, think them monumentally boring. It was a sweet way to end each day. Not as sweet as being in bed together, but nice.

"I think about you when I'm moving around, doing my routine stuff," Grant said.

"Oh, you do not."

"I do. At the espresso bar this morning, I wondered what if you were with me, and what you'd think of the weirdos standing in line ahead of me."

"I like weirdos," I said, a tad defensively. "Anyway, tell me more. What'd you do at work today?"

Grant had described his small but bustling office – I felt I already knew the two women and one guy who worked for him – efficient and steady, yet easy-going and fun with plenty of joking throughout the day. I could also picture his upscale condo apartment on the sixth floor overlooking Elliot Bay, tidy and well-appointed but lived in. And then there was the night life. Grant told me about one or two clubs that he used to go to, usually with a group of friends or to hear a particular performer. But he felt too old for those places now, he said.

"Well, I'm not. You *will* take me out to hear some good music when I come up, won't you? I'd love to hear some great blues in a dark, intimate little bar like I've seen in the movies. Do they really have those?"

"Yeah, there's a few left, if you know where to look."

"You know where to look, I have no doubt. I want to hear someone like J.B. Hutto, or James Cotton, the old guys. Are they still alive?"

"You've missed Hutto by a few decades, but James Cotton's still alive. He was here awhile back, but I think he's too big to play 'intimate' clubs anymore. You could see him at Bumbershoot – he plays there sometimes."

"What's Bumbershoot?"

"It's this huge festival at Seattle Center every Labor Day. Lots of international music and arts. It's got everything. Want to come? You'd love it."

"Maybe. Sounds fun, but crowded. You'll still have to take me to a small nightclub in the bad part of town."

"Okay, fine. But you may have to settle for some of the newer blues men, like Too Slim or Robbie Laws. They're good, and even better, they're still alive."

"Whatever you say, Kemo Sabe. You're the one who's got his finger on the pulse." I gave myself a mental high-five for my cleverness at slipping in the nickname. True, I'd mooched it from Travis but Grant didn't have to know that.

"Oh, yeah," he laughed. "You want to know what's hip n' happenin' in Downtown Seattle, I'm all over it."

We could joke and talk about what we'd do when I got to Seattle, but we both knew it wasn't going to happen any time soon. There was no way I could leave the Bluffs during the high season. From a financial point of view, skipping more than a day here and there was about all I could get away with until the winter, probably October, when things slowed down. Grant had the straight, not to mention better paying, five-day-a-week job. So if we were going to get together before then, more hands on, face to face and belly to belly, he was going to have to come to me.

With the summer heating up and the golfers coming to town in droves, life in the caddie shack had gotten more exciting. There wasn't much time to get bored or even carry on a conversation. We had as much work as we could handle, which was a good thing, but exhausting. At any rate the busy pace meant I couldn't stay in a funk missing Grant all day.

It took half a week for me to catch up with Tucson Johnny, and I barely had a chance to get him filled in on the Rocks rumor before he got an assignment for a double-bagger. After

I explained the payback planned for Rocks, Johnny said, "No problem." Exactly the response I expected. With his help it wouldn't be long before I'd be seeing Rocks with a few new tics, looking over his shoulder and sweating in public. It's times like these when I really appreciate the team spirit of small-town folks.

But the big news circulating around the resort was about the upcoming charity tournament. We'd all seen the posters and heard management honchos tooting their horns about it for days. I didn't notice any of the caddies sharing in the excitement, until Larson announced it one morning to everyone in the shack, preparing us for a day off.

"I want to remind you all that August first is the charity tournament, which will play the Bluffs loop. So, since the Hollows will be the only course open to the paying public, there's limited caddie work that day," Larson said. "Instead, some of you hotshots might want to get sponsors and put together a team. In fact, we'd be disappointed if we didn't see you out there. It'd show your gratitude to the town of Eden, and you might even earn some bragging rights."

That brought a mixed ruckus of pumped fists, scoffs, and snipes.

A guy shouted from the back, "How much will it cost us?" It was one of the transient bag-packers who I recognized but didn't know by name, only that he was always rude and unfriendly. I pegged him as the type who hustled for as many loops as he could get, and then blew thousands at the casino.

Larson answered, "It's a minimum of $100 per player. But you're encouraged to get sponsors to make pledges, and there'll be a prize for the one who brings in the most."

162

The bag-packer evidently wanted no part of that contest. "So besides losing a day's pay, we're supposed to fork over $100." He demonstrated his contempt with a loud snort.

"It's for a good cause," Larson continued, "and I'm sure you drop more than that in ten minutes at the blackjack tables."

Ha! I knew I was right about him.

"The proceeds go to the Eden Beach Community Swimming Pool Fund, and Singing Bluffs Resort is waiving greens fees for this event. It's a big deal, a way for the Bluffs to give something back to the community. Dig deep and see if you slackers can find some generosity in yourselves. If you don't play, help out as scorekeepers, officials, or offer to caddie *gratis* for a player who doesn't know the course or can't pack a bag for eighteen." He paused and gave a dispassionate look around the room. "Join in, it'll be fun."

Then he abruptly turned his attention back to the ever-present clipboard and began calling out assignments. He didn't call one for me so I returned to my Janet Evanovich paperback.

But my mind wandered. It was the tenth or maybe eleventh of July, I think. That meant I had three weeks to decide what to do. Playing was out, because even if I started practicing now I'd only end up embarrassing myself. But caddying might be kicks. I'd never caddied a tournament before, and this would be with just-for-fun, generous, good-hearted folks, not competitive ex-fratboy jocks. I could imagine bagging for a nice grandfatherly type with a good sense of humor. We'd have loads of laughs and donate to a good cause at the same time.

Or – I could take advantage of the compulsory day off, throw in a couple of mental health days of my own, and go see Grant.

THAT AFTERNOON AT the bar, I'd still not made up my mind. During my loop with a returning guest, who didn't need me for anything besides moral support and cleaning his clubs, I flip-flopped twenty times. Clearly, I wouldn't get a better chance to go to Seattle for months. I could probably leave Rover with Gail. I'd only be missing two or three days' pay, and I knew Grant would insist on buying my plane ticket. I could make up the loss of income if I didn't take any more days off between now and then. But what if I get the flu or something? And I really hate not paying my own way, letting Grant foot the bill for my flight and restaurants. If I stay, think of the valuable experience I'd be getting caddying a tournament. And by volunteering I'd be showing the boys in the front office what a dedicated trooper I was. That would score some points for my future. I could also meet some good, fun people, a real bonus. I wanted to stay for the excitement.

And I really wanted to see Grant.

"Hola, Chica. Que pasa?" Travis greeted me when I pulled up the barstool next to him. Twitch was on his other side, and they both looked as if the term *happy hour* was made for them.

"Nada, Dude. I mean Hombre. Where's Jess?" As I sat I noticed Cheryl, the owner's daughter (who only worked if she had to) behind the bar. I asked for a pint of Bud Light and without a word or change of expression, she obliged.

"I already asked. She's off, appointments and whatnot," Travis said.

Twitch held up a finger when Cheryl set a glass in front of me. "Let me buy you one, Sunshine. You look like you've been carrying more than a bag of golf clubs today."

Travis added, "You do look kinda down. Anything we can help with, Sis?"

"You guys are killing me with these nicknames. Thanks for the beer, Twitch." I took a sip as Cheryl turned to note the charge on Twitch's tab, then disappeared into the back of the bar. "I was kind of hoping to get Jess's opinion about something."

Travis mimed a "Well?" with his upturned hands. "Try us. What's the worst that can happen?"

"I hate to think. Okay. Well, there's this tournament thing happening next month at the Bluffs..."

"Yeah, yeah," Travis said. "I'm jazzed. I've got half a dozen sponsors lined up so far."

"Wait. You play golf?"

"Yeah. Why is that so hard to believe?"

"You never told me, that's all."

"There's a lot I haven't told you. Should I also have told you that I can sing all the verses of Dylan's "Subterranean Homesick Blues" in the shower?"

Twitch quietly cleared his throat, then asked, "What's the problem, Lainey?"

I sighed, and gave them the *guy* version of my dilemma, omitting any references to sexual frustration and satisfaction thereof. I didn't expect resolution, but it did help to voice the pros and cons of the situation.

There was a long pause after I finished. Twitch nodded sagely. Travis furrowed his brow. Obviously they were not going to be offering any solutions.

"Forget about it," I said, letting them off the hook. "I'll figure it out. There's time. I don't have to decide today."

Their faces brightened, and they sipped their beers in unison.

"Yeah, I like to golf when I get the chance," Travis said, letting the conversation about my problem disappear into thin air. "Of course, I don't play at Screaming Bluffs – can't afford those greens fees."

"So you play at the muni course?" I asked.

"Yeah. I played a couple times with Stewart when I first got here, and I got to know a few guys. So now I'm part of a regular foursome on Wednesdays."

Twitch said, "The muni is a damn fine golf course. I remember when it first opened up, back in '63 I believe. But it was only a 9-hole course then. Hardly worth the effort. Then it changed hands and the new owners put in the back nine. I think it was 1973. They call it a par 72 but I think it's rated wrong. I regularly got a 70, and I wasn't that good."

I caught myself staring at him and covered my astonishment by ducking behind Travis and taking a drink. I was trying to imagine this frail oldster swinging a golf club without falling. His weight was probably less than his age.

Travis's analysis went a different way. "So you probably hit your age, back in the day."

"Yep, back in the day." Twitch smiled.

"I'm doing okay, myself," Travis continued. "My buds call me Tiger."

166

"Oh, yeah," I said, having recovered enough to move on. "You're Travis Woods. I get it."

"No relation. I'm taller," he said with a straight face. "Anyway, that's how I knew about the tourney at the Bluffs. The guys I play with want to stake me, and they've been getting pledges lined up."

"Can't beat that," I said. "That's really nice. You must be good."

"Well, I won't be in the running for low score, but I might bring home a prize, like for straightest drive, or KP or something."

Newbie that I was, I hadn't yet bothered to learn tournament lingo. Good thing I was amongst friends. "What's KP?" I asked.

"Closest to the pin," Travis said. When I gave him a puzzled look, he added, "I know, it's lame, but that's what they call it on the West Coast. KPs are set up on one of the par 3s, and they pick par 5s for the longest drive, and in some tournaments there's also a prize for straightest drive. In charity tournaments, the prizes are usually things like gift baskets, or golf jackets. You know, items donated by local merchants. The only cash prizes for this tourney will be for low team scores."

"How much are we talking about?" I asked.

"I don't think they've announced it yet, but it won't be much. From what I understand, they don't expect a huge draw. It's mostly to give us locals a chance to play out there and raise funds for the pool. If my team does win any money, I'd donate my half back. And if I win any gift baskets, I gotta share with my golf buddies. That's the deal." He grinned. There must have been a funny story in there somewhere. I tried to picture baskets of teas and bath salts divvied up with his guys at the muni. Okay, that would be funny.

"Who's your partner?"

The one thing I had gleaned from the posters was that the tournament format would be "Alternate Shot" which called for two-person teams. That much I'd learned from a golf magazine I picked up in the caddie shack. Each hole would have four players at a time, like a regular foursome, except with only one ball for each team. The first player per team hits the drive, the second player hits the second shot, the first player hits the third shot, and so on until the ball is holed. Sounded like a true trust-your-buddy situation to me.

"I don't know yet," Travis replied. "We're looking for someone who can pony up his own entry fee, because the guys want to pool all the pledges on just me. They're trying for the prize for the most money pledged. They don't even know what the prize is," he laughed. "It's just the challenge of the thing."

These guys must be a riot.

"Anyway, I've got to declare by Thursday. If I don't find someone soon, I'll get paired up with someone else who doesn't have a team. It's the luck of the draw."

We sat silent a moment, each absorbed in our own thoughts. Me, I was taking in the ambiance of Pappy's Tavern. Beer, shop-talk, crappy music, the clicking of pool balls – who could ask for more?

"Grant," Twitch said.

I said, "What?" at the same time that Travis said, "Who?"

Twitch was still looking at the wall behind the bar, and I don't think he'd moved a muscle in ten minutes. In his soft, wispy voice he said, "Grant would be your partner."

168

Travis said, "Wow, that would be so cool. He's a nice guy. And he's played out there, right Lainey? I'll bet he's a bitchin' golfer. Would you ask him? See if he'll come down for the tournament, instead of you going up there, and voilà! – your problem's solved, my problem's solved. We kill two birdies with one golf ball."

Twitch's whole body jiggled up and down, his silent, signature laugh when something really tickled him. I got up from my barstool, went over to him, took hold of his chin and gave him a soft kiss on the cheek.

"Hey, what about me?" Travis asked.

I put my hands behind his head, drew his lips to mine, and laid one on him.

CHAPTER 18

"WOW. I'M SURPRISED the resort would hold a charity tournament in the middle of the high season. Nice."

I waited for Grant to continue, my cell phone pressed to my hot little ear.

After an eternity, he said, "Well, let me see... another golf trip to Eden... checking my calendar... yes, I think I can swing it. No pun intended, but funny, no?"

"No. Get serious, Grant. Are you sure this is something you want to do?"

"Are you kidding? Like I need an excuse to come see you? It's perfect."

"Okay," I said, "but listen. Maybe I really don't need to stick around for the tournament. It's not a big deal. Probably just a bunch of townies getting their asses kicked by resort regulars." Just saying the words put a sympathetic lump in my throat. "I could miss it, go to Seattle instead. I really do want to. It's just that..."

"I know, and we'll get you here someday. Don't worry about it, Babycakes. I'll come to Eden this time and it'll be fun. You know I love a good game."

"But I feel bad that it's another long drive for you, for such a short stay, and I'd hate it if taking you away from work hurt your business." Why did it sound like I was trying to talk him out of it? In a flash, I realized that I was being nagged by a guilty conscience. I took a second to congratulate myself on my budding maturity.

"Lainey, we have to see each other. I don't care about the drive, and my business gets along fine without me. I don't know about you, but this long-distance thing is killing me." He sighed.

"I know. Me too." I repeated his sigh. "We just have to cope until... I don't know... until one of us moves. Does that sound crazy?"

"Hey, we're young. Crazy is part of the definition."

I knew Grant was avoiding the issue, but for the moment that was fine by me.

"You remember Travis, don't you?" I asked.

"Uh, yeah. I think I met him at Gail's party, her nephew or something. Yeah, I remember him. Seemed like a nice guy."

I was grateful that he didn't mention the drunken encounter with Travis and the bimbo after the fireworks. That impression was probably best forgotten when considering a partner for a golf match.

"Well, he's gonna be in the tournament and he wanted me to ask you if you'd be his team partner."

"How's his game?" he asked.

"I've never seen him play, but he's got a good rep at the muni course."

He laughed. "Uh oh. I hope I can keep up with him."

"You're sweet. You know that?" I was smiling so big my jaw hurt.

ROVER AND I went to the south jetty after my loop on Wednesday for a little together time. I'd been ignoring him lately, lost in my own rollercoaster world of self-doubts and high expectations. I watched him root around the driftwood, chase birds, and bark just for the hell of it, like he does every single time we come to the beach.

When will I ever learn to follow his example? Take life as it comes, and let things fall into place. Rover knows. Mom knows. Gail knows. And everybody I can think of who tries to advise me knows. Except Jessica. She's usually way off.

I spotted a guy walking towards us along the shoreline. He was wearing white painter pants rolled up to his knees and dirty sneakers that were tied together and hung over his shoulder, like the kids on postcards. As he got closer I could see that this kid had a beard. I recognized Travis at the same time he recognized us.

"Hey! It's my favorite pooch." He knelt in the wet sand to let Rover lick his face, oblivious to what that did to his pant legs. "Cut it out, you little shit. You're getting slobber all over my glasses." He smiled up at me. "And you brought your human with you. Hey, Shortstuff."

"Hi, guy. What are you doing bumming on the beach? It's Wednesday. Aren't you supposed to be on the golf course with your boyfriends?"

"We played this morning. It's too late in the day now to start a new landscaping job, and the beach beckoned. I do get some time off, you know."

"Good. Then come on, walk with me."

Travis stood up and we continued down the beach the way he had come, a strong wind at our backs. I was remembering the impulsive kiss I'd given him at Pappy's, and a guilty feeling niggled at me. Quick, Tidwell, duck and cover.

"Hey, I talked to Grant last night. He said he'd be here to play the tournament with you."

"Very cool. I'll sign us up tomorrow. Now I don't have to sweat partnering with some doofus, or worse, someone who will think I'm a doofus." He stopped in his tracks. "He doesn't, does he?"

"I don't know. It didn't come up," I said with a straight face, but then relinquished a smile. "No. He likes you."

He jabbed a fist at my bicep and we picked up our pace.

Travis said, "If you walk as far as the viewpoint where I parked the truck, I'll give you a lift back. Otherwise you'll have a hell of a time walking into this wind. Don't you get tired of it, especially after walking a loop packing a forty-pound bag? What are those courses out there, about seven miles?"

"About. It was rough the first few weeks, but I'm used to it now. Walking here without having to carry anything feels good, like I'm floating." That was true, although I'd never put it into words before.

Travis said, "Yeah, I know what you mean. Where I worked in Silverton, sometimes I had to carry a backpack of tanks, to spray pesticides, herbicides, whatever. They must've weighed sixty pounds starting out. Do that for six hours and when you unstrap that sucker it's 'Flight Control, we have lift off.'"

I laughed and we kept walking. I felt an easy companionship with Travis, not something I'd experienced with very many guys. There was no sexual tension, no wondering who would make the first move, and when. No bullshit. Just two people who'd discovered that they share the same interests. Like two antisocial Trekkies finding each other at a ten-year class reunion. Or a bridesmaid and a best man who'd never met, finding out that they were both hardcore Giants fans.

Simpatico, man, as Travis would say.

"So, at the tourney, what's your role?" he asked. "You're going to double-bag for us, aren't you?" He gave my back a slap. It was a good ol' boy kind of slap, only softer.

"Forget it, buster. You're both big boys. You can carry your own bags, and Grant knows the course and can give you tips. What I'm going to do, I think, is offer to bag for somebody who's never played there. If I ask real nice, I can get the caddie master to put me with a team playing against you guys."

"Sweet. I can't wait to see the layout of this place. Everything I've read about it says it's phenomenal."

"You haven't gone out there?" I asked. "You can see the first tee and most of the eighteenth hole of both courses from the lodge."

"I haven't had the time. I've seen the photos on their website is all. But you can't really appreciate the slopes and contours from pictures. I want to be able to get the full effect.

174

There's more to a golf course than you might think. There should be perspective, a visual rhythm from tee box to horizon."

"Spoken like a true landscaper," I laughed.

Travis smiled sheepishly. "My dream job is to someday design a golf course."

"Get out!"

"Well, not design one, but be the landscaping contractor for a course designer."

"Wow, you? You could landscape a golf course?"

The look he gave me revealed that I'd offended him.

"I'm sorry, Travis. I didn't mean to say it's not like I think you couldn't, or I mean I think you could... I mean, I'm sure you could." Stupid mouth.

"I'm not just a yard maintenance guy, you know." His tone was defensive. "I worked for the landscaper in Silverton for five years, took the exam and now I'm licensed. My business is insured and bonded. I just have to mow lawns, stuff like that, to build up clientele. Once I'm better known, I can advertise and compete for new construction jobs, putting in whole systems."

"And someday, a golf course," I said with more oomph, to make up for my previous mangled mess.

"Yeah, well, someday."

"Who knows? Maybe someone will put in another golf course around here. Since the Bluffs opened, Eden is making a name for itself as a golfer's paradise. The area could use another course."

"I may have to look around, go up north. But I hope not. I like it here," he said.

We walked on. The wind had settled down, which made the droning of the ocean and the cries of the seagulls more distinctive. Rover and I walked on the wet sand, and Travis was still letting the waves wash over his feet.

"You know what we ought to do?" Travis said as we turned to make our way up the dune to the parking lot. "Let's go get Jess and go out to dinner. On me."

"How come? Did you win a lottery or something?"

"No, but on Wednesdays you can get 'Early-bird Specials' at the Holiday Inn, if we hurry. I'll run you back to your Jeep, you go pick up Jess at Pappy's, and I'll go ahead and get a table."

"Sounds good to me."

JESS WAS JUST getting off her shift when I walked in the door. She said, "Hell, yeah," as soon as I mentioned dinner. She grabbed her coat and purse, then cocked her head and jutted her chin towards the Twitch end of the bar. Instead of Twitch, I saw Rocks sitting there, alone, nursing a beer. When he noticed me, he gulped the last bit and left out of the side door.

"How long had he been there?" I asked as we pulled out of the lot.

"Half an hour or so. He's been coming in early afternoons, always by himself, and stays for just one beer."

"I wonder if he's working very much. It's really weird that I haven't seen him for a few days."

"I asked him, 'how's it going?' and he told me he'd been taking it easy lately due to a 'pulled rotator cuff.' His usual running partners say 'hi' to him when they come in, but no one sticks around. There's no smart-mouthed lip, no

176

perverted leering at the girls, no loud obnoxious laugh. It's just not the same ol' Rocks," she said with a smirk. "I actually like him better now that he's a crack dealer."

"Are any of the hard-core dudes asking about him?"

"Curly said they were. I don't usually see the zombies during my shift, just your everyday tweakers, and they're not even talking to him. Get this – Curly told me he'd heard that Rocks is a nark, and that's why everyone is treating him like he's got the T-Virus."

I laughed, only sort-of getting the joke. Knowing that Jessica and Curly are gamers, I guessed that the T-Virus was something from a video game and, therefore, beyond me.

"Anyway, Lain, let's not let that douchebag spoil our fun. Drive faster. I'm starving."

CHAPTER 19

THINGS WERE HEATING up at Singing Bluffs Resort. In the literal sense, the weather was finally starting to feel like summer, which meant on most days you could count on the sun being out and the high temperatures approaching seventy. Of course, those were also the days that the north wind was strong enough to blow you out of your socks, so seventy degrees felt like forty.

But there was a different heat coming out of the caddie shack. The loudmouths complained that the tournament wasn't fair. Only the caddies assigned to the Hollows would get a fee that day, and Larson made sure he saved those spots for non-complaining caddies. Those caddies then got raked over the coals when Larson was out of sight. Back-biting was worse than usual, and those of us who wanted to be part of the tournament were catching flak for being ass-kissers. The fun was going right out of this thing.

Resort bigwigs were hyping the hell out of the charity tournament, updating press releases, tacking posters to any vertical surface that had empty space, and pulling strings with every merchant in town. Eden felt like a company town where every able-bodied person worked for chits with the resort logo on them. I couldn't get out of the grocery store without hearing at least four conversations about the tournament. Even the sign in front of the Presbyterian church said, "*Charity Begins at Home – And Continues at Singing Bluffs Golf Resort.*"

The one place I could count on to ignore the hoopla was Pappy's Tavern. Golfers and caddies alike went about their business there hardly mentioning it at all. The business first and foremost was drinking. Then came bullshitting. The tournament might come into a conversation once in a while under the bullshitting category, but only briefly. Our positions were pretty well known to all, whether we were players, collaborators, or opponents. There wasn't any point in arguing when there was drinking to be done.

The main thing Grant and I talked about was being together again. I had no anxiety about his pending arrival this time. I had plenty of a more physical discomfort though. It was all I could do to get through each day without stumbling over my own legs. My pelvis had taken control and the rest of my body had to just follow along, like a sightless animal with an innate reproductive desire searching for its mate. Eew.

Talking to him on the phone every night gave me nominal satisfaction, but at least I could get some sleep. I got up every morning, went to the course, and spent the day with a population of definitely inferior male specimens. The benefit though, was that without my previous tendency to let a cute guy distract me, I could focus on the ball more. My *caddie's eye* was improving and I was becoming the golfer's guru.

My prowess not only brought in better tips, it upped my status in the caddie shack. Guests turned in rating cards that gave me high marks. Larson and his boss, the course supervisor, noticed and I was given a bag on a more regular basis than the rest of the first-years in the bucket. There were jealous grumblings from a few slackers, but I felt I'd earned respect from the rest of the crew.

Although Rocks was back at work, he was not among the grumblers. In fact, he hadn't hassled me or anyone else since the rumor started, and I'd kind of lost track of the mess he was in. Admittedly, I breathed a tiny sigh of relief that he wasn't in jail, or dead.

My sense of composure didn't last long. A few days later I was sitting in the best cushiony chair in the shack waiting for an assignment, deeply engrossed in the Agatha Christie paperback I'd found at the Laundromat, which was my neighborhood's lending library of moldy mysteries. A sudden commotion of caddies made me look up in time to see a county sheriff's patrol car parking out front. The shack emptied of the usual suspects before the deputy shut his car door. I was only mildly interested, so I kept half an eye on Larson's office while I continued reading. After ten minutes, the deputy drove off and Larson came into the main room.

Most of the senior caddies had gone out at the first tee-times, and, what with the recent departure of deadbeat dads, etc., there was barely a dozen of us left. Larson held a sheet of paper and scanned the room.

"Listen up. News bulletin from the front office," he said with more severity than usual.

We looked at each other nervously, not knowing whether to laugh or not. Larson had never sounded like an executive before.

"In preparation for the fundraising event, Bluffs management is looking at ways to show the community that they... I mean, we... are in step with the good citizens of Eden Beach."

Well, that shouldn't be too hard, I thought.

"Along those lines, it's been something of an embarrassment to them... I mean, us... that whenever the local county Mounties drive up," his voice getting louder and edgier with every word, "there's a bunch of our contracted associates bailing out the back windows!"

He took a moment to gather himself. I could tell that this was hard for him.

"So, here's what they did."

Oops. He was definitely having trouble with this we/they thing.

"The decision was made to work in conjunction with the sheriff's office, to open up the lines of communication, shall we say."

No one moved. I think we'd all stopped breathing.

"Now, I'm gonna repeat this to the other guys as they come in off their loops, and I want you all to tell your buddies – the ones that flew the coop a few minutes ago," he said with a pointed glare at the windows. "The deputy just handed over this list of names," he shook the sheet of paper, almost shredding it in the process, "names of people he called 'persons of interest.'

"As caddie master, it's my job to see that every bum on this list gets all the encouragement he needs to contact the authorities and have a little chat. To help them along, I'll be making sure they have plenty of time to do just that. If your name's called – or if you hear the name of one of your cohorts, you might want to pass along this message: Don't bother showing up here until you get a clearance from the sheriff."

Larson read names for a full minute. Half of them I'd never heard of, at least by their legal names. I was about to sink back into my soft chair and my book when I saw Corky jump as he heard one of the names, and whisper a startled, "Rocks!" to Tick.

This could not be good. As far as I knew, Rocks had never been in this kind of trouble before. I realized then that he had been one of the fugitives, and that was a first. In other "raids" I'd witnessed, Rocks had stayed front and center with the wisecracks, loud as ever, laughing at his own stupid jokes about the deadbeats and druggies.

Uh oh. Great, Tidwell. You've gotten a poor innocent schmuck canned for no good reason. What if he had a wife and kids and they ended up homeless and starving because Daddy lost his job? But I knew that no woman was stupid enough to marry Rocks, so I was safe there. And he's not really innocent, he's a creep. Just not so creepy that the cops would have anything on him.

The problem was that he wouldn't be getting work again by telling them what they wanted to hear because he didn't know anything. The druggies and pushers weren't talking to him because they thought he was a nark, and the straights weren't talking to him because they thought he was a user. He was screwed. But was that *my* fault? If he hadn't told guests that I put out, I wouldn't have spread the rumor that he was trying to score drugs. Besides, I wasn't totally to blame for that. Jessica helped.

I took a deep breath, and stood up. I noticed that the other caddies had grouped into four different encampments, each murmuring their own takes on the situation. I flashed back to my third-grade class when Mrs. Osborne told us we all had to stay in at recess because no one would tell who took the candy bar out of her desk. Then, like now, it was a long, lonely walk to the principal's office.

"Uh, Mr. Larson? Could I talk to you for a minute?" I said as I walked in through his open doorway.

"A minute, Tidwell, that's it. I'm kinda busy here," he said without taking his eyes off the computer screen.

He was not his usual good-natured self, and I felt my stomach and my tongue knot up simultaneously.

A quick glance into the caddie room told me no one had noticed. I stepped in, shutting the door behind me.

"It's about Rocks," I managed.

"Oh, crap. What's he done now?"

"No, he hasn't done anything. Lately. It's kind of a long story..."

"Lainey," he looked at his watch and gave me the hurry-up signal.

"Okay. He told Mr. Tiller that I, uh... you know... put out if the tips were right, and Jess and I thought he shouldn't get away with ruining my reputation like that, so we started a rumor about him – Rocks, not Mr. Tiller – and let him see how it felt."

Larson was frozen in place, eyeing me with a frightened look. I paced back and forth in the three feet between his desk and the door.

"So, the rumor was that Rocks was trying to buy some hard drugs in town, and would pay an outlandish price, so the dealers were working him, and since he really wasn't looking to buy from them, because he didn't want the women who he tried to pick up to think he was a lousy lay because he was a tweaker, *and* I don't think he uses anyway, he tried to avoid the dealers, and somehow things got all twisted around and people started calling him a nark, which doesn't even make sense, I *know*, because, if he was a nark he wouldn't be avoiding them, he'd be trying to make contact. Wouldn't he? I'm guessing. I mean, I don't really know how these things work."

I stopped pacing and gripped the edge of his desk in a desperate attempt to get to the point.

"You can't punish him, Mr. Larson, for something he didn't do. Please put him back on the roster and don't make him go have a chat with the sheriff."

Larson's two-way radio, which was lying on the desk right under my nose, squawked. I let out a scream, which made Larson jump and he knocked his clipboard, which went crashing into the wall.

"God damn it!" He picked up the clipboard in one hand and the radio in the other. Pressing the button he said, "Go ahead."

A voice said, "Paulson's party – on their way to Hollows. Tee-time 8:30. You got two available?"

"Got it. Two on their way," he said, fumbling the clipboard and radio while he opened the door and stuck his head out. He brought it back in and shut the door again.

"Tidwell, Rocks has been a pain in the ass to you since you started here. He doesn't deserve any favors."

"But..." I started.

"But, I appreciate you coming to me with this and I'll see what I can do." Larson smiled. "You know, though, that if he gets back on the roster right away, everyone will really think he's a nark, that he ratted."

"Oh, shit," was all I could say.

"It will be interesting to see how he gets out of this one," he said, nodding with satisfaction as he went through the door. "Yes, it just might do him some good."

He strode out into the caddie room, shouting, "Tidwell! Sutherland! Snap to. Head out to the Hollows. Foursome, two guests requesting caddies."

CHAPTER 20

BY THE TIME Grant arrived I was a new woman. Of course it didn't happen all at once. There were several versions of the old woman, then there was the weird woman, and the woman I wouldn't want to be with on a road trip. The feeble, soul-cleansing speech I'd given Larson had triggered impulses I didn't know I had. I cleaned my house more times than I want to admit (if my mother knew, she'd worry that I'd been turned into a Stepford Wife). I bought new bed sheets, cleaned the refrigerator and stocked the kitchen with a fresh supply of easy-to-fix food and beverages, and brushed Rover so many times he quit speaking to me.

My positive attitude carried over to the golf course, where I was uncharacteristically cool, calm, and collected. I somehow managed to keep my mouth in check, and my goodwill extended to all. More than once I tidied up the shack without being prodded. Larson held me up as a good example to the rest of the troops. Those who hadn't known me before ignored this, and the ones who had gave me crude advice about where

I could stick my positivity. I didn't let them bother me though, because my heart was pure.

And, very soon, I was going to get laid by the sexiest man alive.

Meanwhile, we caddies were doing our best to stay clear of the frenzied preparations in the days before the golf tournament. There were strange people coming and going everywhere. All of them had beer guts, but it was easy to tell the difference between the Community Pool Committee members and the resort muckety-mucks. The muckety-mucks all wore regulation Singing Bluffs windbreakers, powder blue with the logo of a yellow seagull on a pink mountain. What is it about golf that says "pastel"?

On Friday I left the Bluffs after an achingly long loop with a group of snotty golf pros from some high-ranking PGA resorts. These guys were whiny momma's boys who'd obviously never played fairways of hard, bump-and-run turf where strategies had to change with the elements. They spent the entire day blaming their clubs, their lies, the other golfers, the grass, the sun, the birds, their CADDIES! Jake and I coddled these brats as much as we could, and when we got to the clubhouse they paid us our fee and a measly $25 tip without so much as a thank you. Give me uncouth, fat, balding windbags from the Midwest any day. At least they show some respect.

To ease the pain, I headed straight for Pappy's.

After a couple hours, maybe more, of the usual R and R with Jess, Travis, and other chumps who I can beat at pool, I made my careful way home to bed. I still hadn't decided whether to go to work in the morning, the day before the tournament. My cell phone registered a missed call from

Grant, but there was no message. That told me he was either on his way, or held up with clients and wouldn't be able to leave Seattle until morning. I didn't want to be on the course when he got here and have him waiting for me, so I wanted to take the day off. But with Sunday being a no-pay day, I knew I really should get in another loop. My resolution, sleep on it.

I realized someone was in my bedroom not a second before I felt an arm pinning me by the shoulders. I smelled coffee breath, and a low, hoarse voice said, "Hey, you sweet thang, let's do it."

I rolled away from him and came up on my feet, ready to kick the living shit out of this guy's teeth, or nuts, or whatever I could reach.

"Hold on, Wild Thing! It's me," Grant said, laughing with what I thought was a little too much zeal for the situation.

"Jesus Christ, Grant! You scared me to death. Why'd you do that?"

"Because you left your door unlocked. Let that be a lesson to you."

"Let *this* be a lesson."

I feinted a kick to the nuts. When he flinched, I dove across the bed and tackled him. We ended up on the floor, giggling and smooching. Rover came from the living room and joined in with bounces and yips.

"Oh, yeah, *now* you're awake," I scolded. "Where were you when I needed you? You let just any sorry sack of shit in here, don't you?"

"Yeah, good dog," Grant said. "And I'm not just any sorry sack of shit. I'm the one who loves you and has been waiting for weeks to ravage your bod."

188

"Yeah, well, you can wait until you shower and brush your teeth. How'd you get here so fast? What time is it, anyway?"

"1:30. I left as soon as I got away from the office. I was already packed, so I just drove out of town and kept driving."

He sniffed his armpits. "Pretty raunchy, huh?"

"I've smelled worse."

"I don't want to know," he said as he got up and headed to the bathroom.

Things got better after that.

As it turned out, I did go to the resort in the morning. Late, but I went. My timing was along the lines of Rocks and crew – not quite the crack of noon, but close. Grant said I needed to go and get a bag that would erase the disgusting, leftover taste of the pro-snobs I'd been around the day before. He said, "Go. You'll see. Everything will turn out okay."

I hate it when he says that.

Because, as he predicted, it wasn't a really, really horrible day. But it was hard to keep my mind on my work, and twice I spaced out tending the flag. My guest was a nice guy who I'd bagged for before, and he knew those were rare mistakes for me. I took some razzing, and he had a good round.

I phoned Grant when I was free, and he said he was at the practice range. Since the whole place was in chaos due to the tournament, I threw caution to the prevailing wind and joined him there. Grant had Rover waiting in the car, so I decided walking the dog was a good ruse. Employees at this end of the resort, on seeing a girl and a froofy-looking mutt on a leash watching her boyfriend hit a bucket of balls, wouldn't recognize her as a caddie. And if by chance there were other caddies around and they turned me in for fraternizing with a guest, well... what the hell, Tidwell! Get a grip and quit stressing over stupid rules that everyone but you breaks. Walk the damn dog and relax.

As I approached, Grant sliced three balls, each sailing more than 300 yards. Long, but wrong.

"Oops," I said quietly.

"Yeah, well. You can't have everything," he said as he turned to greet me with those gorgeous green eyes of his.

I beamed in return. "Good attitude. That's exactly what I like about you."

"That's what you like about me? My calm acknowledgment of failure?"

"That, and a few other things. Go ahead, finish. I promise not to criticize."

"Please, help me all you can, Wild Thing. You're the expert," he said as he teed up another ball. This time it went straight as a string.

"Nice," I said.

"See? All you have to do is stand next to me and I'm golden." He teed up and hit another bullet. "You're going to coach me and Travis tomorrow, aren't you?"

"What? No, I'm not doing that. I've got my own player. Mr. Vanlandingham. You guys will be on your own."

"How good-looking is Mr. Vanlandingham?" He gave me a sideways, suspicious look.

Mr. Vanlandingham, I knew from seeing him around town, looked like Mr. Burns from *The Simpsons*, only older.

"He's hot. And he's almost as tall as I am."

Grant's hoot attracted the attention of others practicing nearby and we shushed each other. I left him to finish his

190

bucket, and walked Rover to where he could pee inconspicuously behind some bushes in the parking lot. When I saw Grant was putting his clubs away, I joined him.

"See you at home?" he asked. The ease with which he asked the question sent a little chill down my spine. He looked at the ground, blinking hard. Maybe the sun was in his eyes.

"Sounds good," I answered.

We decided to skip happy hour at Pappy's and dinner at *our* restaurant, Rosaria's. The idea was to fix an easy dinner for ourselves, relax and talk, and then catch up on our sleep. In actuality, the catching up we did had little to do with eating, talking, or sleeping.

CHAPTER 21

THE MORNING SKY promised a clear, calm day as we walked into the Bluffs staging area together. The atmosphere was full-tilt hubbub and I couldn't help but get a contact high from the excited participants. It didn't matter that this was the same place I came to work almost every day of the week. It felt special. This was a crazy collision of my two worlds – the remarkable golf courses of Singing Bluffs and the easygoing townsfolk of Eden Beach.

And there was free pastry.

I helped myself to a raspberry Danish while Grant schmoozed with the golf pro, and I scanned the crowd for Travis. He was just leaving the sign-in table and heading my way.

"Hey, Stretch, this is a blast. Isn't it?" he said before popping a mini muffin into his mouth.

"Yeah, I know. I can't believe how many people are here. How many teams are there?"

"Forty. A lot of these people are here for the show. It's a big deal, I guess. Like me, they haven't seen this course before."

"So, there'll be like a gallery?" I asked. "I hadn't realized that."

"Especially at the money hole."

"What's the money hole?"

"No. 17, I think." He paused. My blank expression must have indicated my wish for more info because he continued. "It's the hole-in-one hole. All players get a shot at it. The prize is a season of free golf."

"Here?" I was surprised that the Bluffs had ponied up for such an extravagance. I know a hole-in-one is improbable, but still. Could happen.

Just then two middle-aged women came from behind the snack table, refilling the fruit plate and napkin stacks.

"That's right," one answered. "They're taking bets right over there." She pointed out a table where some girls were pushing raffle tickets and a guy was recording something in a tablet. Two big jars were getting stuffed with money. "Each bet placed on the player who makes the hole-in-one wins a free round of golf. It's all going to the swimming pool fund," she beamed.

The other woman held out a plate of apples and bananas. "Make sure you get some fruit, kids. You'll need it to make that lucky shot," she kidded.

I was startled for a moment, before I realized that they didn't know I was a caddie. Since caddies weren't actually representing the resort, we didn't have to wear our whites. In my street clothes I was blending in, just one of the players. I put an apple in my pocket.

Grant came up to us and gave Travis a good ol' boy handshake, their left hands punching each other's shoulders.

"Travis, my man. Ready to kill?"

"Locked and loaded," Travis answered, adding some weird kind of animal noise.

"Oh, for crisesakes. Are you guys going to do this all day?" I asked. "You're embarrassing me."

Travis ignored me and said, "Hey, Grant, when I signed us up, they asked for our team name. I had to make one up on the spot. Hope you don't mind. We're 'Rover's Dream Team.'"

Grant groaned.

I said, "Aww. That's so cute. Thanks, Travis."

"Yeah, cute," Grant said. "That's just what we want to be. Cute."

I left them to their strategizing and went in search of my player. The volunteer at the sign-in table told me Mr. Vanlandingham had signed in with his partner, Buzz Inskeep, pretty early and said they were heading to the practice range.

"What's their team name?" I asked out of curiosity.

She checked the spreadsheet. "The Pork Bellies."

"You're kidding."

"No, that's what they told me. I take it they're some kind of day traders or something," the woman said politely. I thought she was giving them way too much benefit of the doubt. More likely, they took the name from their favorite thing on the breakfast menu at the Garden.

I moseyed around the starting area, chatting with people I recognized. Some of the locals who didn't know me asked whether I was playing and seemed surprised when I said I was caddying.

"But you're such a tiny little thing," the nice people said. Some went so far as to add that I seemed too sweet to be a caddie. My mom should hear that.

It was true that caddies had gotten themselves a bad rap around Eden. The fly-by-night caddies had a habit of leaving unpaid bills when they abruptly split to follow another dream job. The single guys liked to make their presence known wherever they went, flashing wads of cash and making complete asses of themselves. Locals were tired of their loudmouth insolence and showing it. I'd witnessed firsthand some anti-caddie treatment by merchants and landlords. Even though responsible caddies like me outnumber the creeps, it's the creeps who draw the attention.

I had to hand it to Bluffs management – this charity tournament was a good start to bringing townspeople around. To do my part, I put on my sweetest smile and walked among the newcomers, greeting them like they'd just stepped off the tour bus.

"Hi, folks, welcome to Singing Bluffs. I'm Lainey, one of the caddies who works here. Is this your first visit? What do you think of this beautiful setting?"

What a charmer. Bluffs ought to hire me as a full-time hostess. No, wait. Skip that. All that smiling was already hurting my face.

Grant and Travis found me and we went over to check out the prize table. I politely refused the teenage girls' entreaties to buy raffle tickets. Wine and cheese baskets and hand-carved putters were not my thing. Grant was nice enough to buy $10 worth. There was a short line of people handing over $20s to the guy at the table, and he was writing down each bettor's choice for hole-in-one winner. Some golfers standing around were goading their buddies, claiming they were a good bet. I recognized them. They weren't.

Behind the pro shop there was a huge whiteboard lined with a graph for updating scores as they came in. One of the volunteers posting team names was Rocks. He was too busy to notice me, which would've probably embarrassed him. I know he'd been a real asshole to me, but who was I to say 'once an asshole, always an asshole'? Whether he had volunteered just to keep his job or he really wanted to help the community, I had to give him credit. Once the jerks who boycotted the event heard about it, he was going to take a huge ration of ribbing, not to mention the heat he'd feel for the sheriff-chat thing. I envisioned what their faces would look like when I spoke up to defend him.

"So, Twinkle Toes, where are your old codgers?" Travis asked me.

The nickname must have been too *overfriendly* for Grant, because he immediately put his arm around me and kissed the top of my head.

Sweet, but I'm busy here.

"I think that's them over by the carts."

"Carts?" Travis asked. "I thought this was a walk-only course."

"It is," Grant said, "but they have some around for the marshals and groundskeepers. Today they're using them to transport us to the distant holes for the shotgun start. Those two rubes are probably trying to make a deal with the marshal, kicking tires and asking about the mileage."

196

"Be nice, you two. Since you're going to be playing these gentlemen for the day, you should probably try to show some respect, and at least pretend to be gentlemen yourselves," I said with a huff of disgust. I wasn't really mad, just giving them something to worry about. It was, after all, a competition. And I wanted my team to win. "Let's go meet them."

As we approached I got a better look at my champs. Mr. Inskeep appeared to be a fit sixty-something but, when I introduced myself, saying I was their caddie for the day, he immediately admitted being a mediocre duffer with poor eyesight.

"We'll be needing your expert advice, young lady," he said. "Don't be shy about telling us how to improve our shots. Or telling me where my ball is."

Mr. Vanlandingham chuckled, a wheezy, squeaky sound that startled me at first. His high-pitched voice took some getting used to, but the expression on his beaming face was contagious. He reminded me of Twitch and I wondered if they knew each other. I grinned, imagining myself sitting at Pappy's, having a beer with the two of them.

"My girl," he said, "we appreciate any help you have to offer. I don't expect to win but I want to get a better score than some other fellows I know. I've got money riding on this game."

He winked at me and gave another wheezy chuckle.

"I won't let you down, Mr. Vanlandingham."

"Now, now. It's going to be a long day and we don't want to make it any longer by using my atrociously long name. I'm Tom, and this here is Buzz."

"Very glad to meet you. I'm really looking forward to being at your service." I turned to include Travis and Grant. "This is the team we're matched up with today."

Everyone shook hands. Buzz gave Travis the once-over and said, "I saw 'Woods, T' on the scoreboard, and I was a little worried. I'd heard they get some famous players out here."

"No relation. I'm taller," Travis said matter-of-factly. "I'm Travis. I've never played here either so we're on equal terms on that point. This guy's the one to watch out for."

Grant gave a dismissive wave of his hand. "Forget about it. Let's mount up."

He and Travis took off in one of the carts, and I loaded my team's bags in the other. Mr. Magoo chose to drive, Mr. Burns got shotgun, and I hopped on the back. Team Pork Bellies was off and running.

Near the turn stand at No. 9 there was a place to leave carts and we walked to the tee box on 11, our assigned start. Along the way I saw Jake packing two bags for players on the 10th.

"Nice day so far," he shouted to us across the fairway. "I hope your caddie told you what happens later. I know Mr. Garner knows."

He gave a nod of recognition to Grant. It was nice to see his cheerful face, and I was glad our friendship had advanced to the teasing stage since our first round together.

"Hey," I shouted back. "Don't spoil the surprise."

Tom hurried alongside me and asked, "What happens later?"

I turned so that both he and Buzz could hear me. "You know Eden's summer winds. It will pick up pretty hard on these holes overlooking the ocean, No. 10 thru 14. And 4 and 5 get some of it. We got lucky getting here early, but when we come back to play No. 10 we'll be playing into the fan again."

"What's a little wind, eh, Tom?" Buzz laughed. Of course, they were too enamored with the view and the layout to be bothered. Maybe he had a point. Being no strangers to high winds, they might figure out how to play this course better than the out-of-towners.

All four men began taking their practice swings, while I described the hole.

"It's a short par 3, with a small green surrounded by bunkers. The pin is in the back, so that's 160 yards with no wiggle room."

Travis surveyed the landscape and grinned. "This is amazing. I almost want to screw up so I can make the round last longer."

Grant broke his swing and yelled, "What are you saying? No sandbagging, buddy."

"Lighten up, pardner," Travis said. "I'm with you all the way."

I ignored them and looked to my guest. "What's your poison, sir?"

He handed me the driver he'd been practicing with, a move that showed me a caddie's due respect. "I'm going to fly it right up and over. Please hand me my 5-iron, young *lady*," he said with a wink.

I changed the driver for the iron, wiped it quickly with my towel, and gave it to him with a huge smile. "I gotcha. No *sirs*. Tom it is." This was going to be sweet.

A cannon shot sounded from the direction of the lodge, followed by various enthusiastic shouts from surrounding tee boxes. Travis, Buzz, and even ol' Tom gave a rousing, "Whoo-hoo!" of approval. Grant gave a more subdued, "Yes!" and winked at me.

"Let's do this," he added.

In Alternate Shot competition one guy per team tees off, then the other guy shoots, and yada-yada until the ball is holed. They also have to alternate drives. The Pork Bellies had chosen Tom to tee off first, and Rover's Dream Team went with Travis.

Incredibly, both landed the green.

Tom's slow, methodical style was standard golf-lesson "address the ball" procedure. The ball sailed flat and straight, bounced once and rolled to the high side of the green.

"Nice drive, Tom. It's lying right where you want it," I praised. The others were also appreciative. It was early yet.

Travis's style had less finesse, and his stronger swing meant a smaller club. He used a 7-iron and skied the ball in a nice arc. It stuck the green within twenty feet of the pin, an easy two-putt.

As we walked down the fairway, the three newcomers expressed their awe.

"This is some course, alright," Buzz said, thoroughly enjoying himself. The breeze riffled our shirt sleeves but no one seemed to notice. Grant was the only one who kept his eyes straight ahead, aimed towards the green as if already planning his putt.

He spoke without turning. "Tom, did I hear you say you're a betting man?"

"Well, I don't know if I want that widely spread, but I've been known to put my money where my mouth is."

Buzz laughed. "Oh, it's already well known. By everyone at the clubhouse."

"*That's* where I've seen you," Travis remarked. "You play at the muni course. But not usually Wednesdays, I guess. That's when I'm there."

"We play a couple of times a week, any day," Tom said. "But you'll only see us if you're there before ten. That's when we go for breakfast. We tee off at daybreak."

"Yeah, I'll probably miss that. I did see your names on the bulletin board, the week's low scores."

They stopped at the fringe of the green and I pulled the flag while they studied their lies.

Grant restarted the conversation. "So you guys are pretty good, huh? Care for side bets, say, five bucks a hole?"

His eyes twinkled with an unmistakable mischievousness. Who *was* this cocky bastard? I had no idea he was going to be so competitive just because it was a tournament. He definitely was going to piss me off if he took these sweet old guys to the cleaners.

Buzz and Tom appeared to be thinking seriously for a moment, nodded agreement, and Buzz replied as if he'd recited the line a hundred times.

"How does *ten* bucks a hole sound to you?"

Hoo-boy. Things were going to get interesting.

Grant picked up Travis's drive shot, carefully repairing the deep crater it had left in the carpet, and placed his ball-marker. He studied the ball and gave Travis a disparaging look.

"That's the brand you chose? Really?"

Travis just smiled.

As Buzz readied his putt, I pointed out that the mix of harder turf and shorter grasses here meant fast greens and fairways. He punched it anyway.

"Whoa! I see what you mean." His ball rolled past the hole, finally stopping another eight feet away.

Grant's was the away shot, so he putted next. He sent a nice smooth roll to within six feet, then silently walked back to his bag and replaced his putter.

Travis said, "You're pretty confident I'll make the putt, aren't ya?"

"Nothing to it, partner. It's all yours." He smiled.

I rolled my eyes, again. They were getting a workout.

Tom's putt missed by inches, and they told Buzz to go ahead and tap it in.

Travis said, "Sweet," then sauntered to the marker. He quickly placed his ball, took a casual stance, and with one glance at the hole he made the putt.

My team half-groaned, half-laughed.

"What?" he said innocently. "It's a simple game."

Tom pulled a wad of cash out of his pocket and handed Grant a ten. Grant flashed his cheesy grin and said, "Nice hole, fellas. But wait till you see 12."

He was right. The Bluffs' No. 12 was the Heart Attack Hill of the resort. A long 532 yards and all uphill. It hadn't actually killed anyone yet. I hoped Mr. Vanlandingham wouldn't be the first.

While we waited for the group ahead to clear the fairway, I sidled up to Grant and whispered, "You're not going to take advantage of these sweet old guys, are you?"

"What 'take advantage of'? This is a contest, isn't it? If they didn't want the action they wouldn't have taken it." He smiled at me and then said more loudly, in Travis's direction, "And you can't win if you don't bet. Right, partner?"

Travis raised an eyebrow and bit his lip. "I dunno, pardner. Ten bucks a hole... that's kinda steep."

"Psh. Don't be such a wuss."

When the players ahead had advanced to the green, Grant stepped up to tee his ball.

Travis said, "I hope that's one of those high-priced *designer* balls. Show us how that thing works, dawg."

Grant didn't respond but I could see him stiffen. He took three more practice swings before he set himself at the tee. The drive faded and bounced on the edge of the fairway before rolling into the weeds. He swore, just once.

"I bet that wasn't supposed to happen," Travis said.

Grant said nothing.

As Buzz teed his ball, I said, "You could follow his line, Buzz, and not put as much on it. That way your second shot should easily clear that bunker in the middle."

"Exactly what I was thinking," he said. He drove it nicely, landing it in the middle of the fairway about a hundred yards from the bunker.

"Nice," I said, drawing a glare from Grant. I stuck my tongue out at him.

Tom was away, so he and I walked ahead to their ball. The other three steered towards the high grass on the right to look for Grant's ball.

"They seem like nice young fellas," Tom said as we walked. "I take it they're friends of yours?"

"So far. Check in with me at the end of the day. That could change."

The Pork Bellies were on in four, thanks to my expert advice and my intentionally slow pace to keep Tom breathing. Rover's Dream Team took a stroke because they couldn't find Grant's drive, but they snapped out of it and were on in five.

"This looks like a dance floor, but don't let it fool you," I advised my team. "There's a lot of room and it's got a transverse slope. Tricky."

Buzz was the first to putt. It didn't get enough juice so when it got to the slope, it rolled off away from the hole.

"We can take this hole with a two-putt, Travis," Grant said. "There's no way they can sink it in two."

"Yep. Set it up, Grant."

I noticed the 'partner' BS was missing from their chatter now. That must have been a long walk up the fairway.

Grant's putt rolled two-thirds of the distance to the hole, leaving Travis in fair shape for a double bogey. Unfortunately, Travis missed. Tom learned from that mistake and putted straight, at just the right speed, leaving Buzz nine feet away.

If Grant's shot went in they'd score an eight, otherwise known as the dreaded Snowman. Buzz would have to make his putt to win the hole.

Grant took time lining up his putt, more seriously than I'd ever seen him do it before.

"Just hit the ball, Alice," Buzz teased from the sidelines.

Grant fussed another half a minute and finally took slow aim to give it a smooth tap. It went in the hole and I would've joined the others in saying, "Nice shot," if he hadn't directed a dig at Travis.

"Now that's the way you do it, Farm-boy. Nice and slow. You don't amble up to it, take a poke and hope you get lucky."

Farm-boy? Ouch. I peeked over at Travis to see how he took it. He seemed to be enjoying the scenery again.

Meanwhile Buzz had walked over to the high grass in such a manner that could only be described as *ambling*. He picked a long, dry stem and stuck it in his mouth. Then he *ambled* back to his ball marker, replaced it with his ball, stuck the weed behind his ear and putted. It went in.

Our laughs carried to the next fairway and back down the hill to Jake's group. He gave me a thumbs-up. Even from that distance I was sure he could tell from Grant's body language who was getting dissed.

"How's that, Slick? Did I do that right?" Buzz drawled.

Grant said nothing as he dug into his pocket, and the ten changed hands.

CHAPTER 22

AS THE DAY progressed, I could tell that the locals were having fun with the Scottish type links and the bounce-and-roll turf. Every once in a while we'd hear hoots of happiness from nearby teams. Whether the joy was from well-played shots or remarkably shitty ones, it didn't matter. Folks were enjoying themselves.

When we got to No. 16 we could see a gallery of bystanders around the green. Team Pork Bellies had a good time playing to the crowd, but making lousy putts. Grant and Travis were too intent on their score to pay much attention to the audience. But Travis's chip missed the green, which made Grant bitchy, which made him blow his shot too.

When we finished we realized that the crowd was there mainly to watch the money hole, No. 17. That, and the drink cart was parked there.

The pace of play had slowed considerably because every player got to tee off, in hopes of sinking it. While the five of us stood in line for our beers (I wasn't officially on duty, after all), Travis explained it to me.

"The alternate-shot rules still apply. Whoever's turn it is for teeing off, that's the ball that's played. So, since it's Grant's turn, when I make the hole-in-one it won't count for our score, just the prize. I'll still have to play his ball, from *wherever*."

He grinned at Grant. Grant was silent, but his jaw tightened noticeably and the temperature around us dropped several degrees.

They walked away in different directions and I took my beer off to the side where I could sit down. Tom and Buzz were yakking it up with people in the gallery, finding out who, if anyone, had come close so far. The jokes were flying and I could tell that this had been a profitable location for the drink cart. For such a worthy cause, people were evidently happy to pay the extra bucks as a donation to the swimming pool fund. And from the sound of things, the entertainment alone was worth the price.

While we waited for the teams ahead of us to move on, the team behind us caught up. Jake set his bags down and came over to join me.

"Are we having fun yet?" he asked tiredly.

"It's different, I'll say that."

"I know. My guys aren't taking their game very seriously, but I guess that's to be expected. What about your old-timers – they ham-n-eggin' it?"

I had no idea what the hell that meant, but I said, "Oh, yeah. They are totally ham-n-eggin' it."

"How are Woods and Mr. Garner doing?"

"Their score isn't that bad, but their match play has the Pork Bellies leading five to two. For some reason, Grant is really off his game and getting uptight."

Jake nodded. "Looks to me like Mr. Garner doesn't do so well with competition."

"That can't be it. I've never seen it bother his golf game before."

"I'm not talking about the golf."

Before I could respond the crowd began its migration back to the 17 tee box, indicating that the previous teams had cleared the green and they were ready for new blood. I left Jake and picked up Mr. Vanlandingham's and, for good measure, Mr. Inskeep's bags. Tom and Buzz had finished their beers and were fired up – as fired up as anyone could expect from the Medicare league.

Onlookers parted for me as I walked forward with a ceremonial attitude. The spirit of the moment prompted me to say, "Watch it, my crew's comin' through, and they mean bidnez."

The Pork Bellies had won the previous hole so it was Buzz's turn to lead off.

"The pin's in the back of the green, 203 yards," I advised. "You might want to fly it 180 yards and let it feed into the funnel, which starts front left. But hit it too far to the right and it's bad news. It'll go over a steep ridge and end up in the beach grass."

Buzz already had his 5-iron out and was taking some warm-up swings outside the tee box. He didn't really need to warm up, since we'd been playing for two hours, but the gallery expected it. I hoped he saved some of that action for later.

A man in the gallery called out, "Go for it, Buzz. My money's riding on you."

A few others joined in. "Yeah, Buzz. You can do it."

"Win it for me, Buzz," the first guy yelled.

They quieted down as he addressed the ball, and a yell of "In the hole!" blared out before the club head finished its upward arc. He shanked it, and the ball disappeared over the dreaded ridge. Creative curse words followed, the losing bettor's louder than Buzz's.

Grant got out his new club, which I know cost him a bundle, and he approached the tee box. He looked sexy in his neatly pressed khakis and short-sleeved polo that showed off his biceps. The wind tousled the back of his hair as he studied the distant green. I was lost in adoration when the jeering started.

"Let's go, City Slicker. Show us what you're made of."

"Nice sticks, but you'll need more than that, Pretty Boy."

"Think you've got the right stuff, Hot Shot? I don't. Ten bucks says he shanks it."

"No bet. He'll blow it."

Grant's gaze didn't veer from his target, but I could see the back of his neck turning red, and he seemed to be chewing the inside of his cheek.

"Hey, hey, hey!" It was Travis. "Hold it down. Let the guy take his shot."

Way to go, Travis. That was a nice thing to do for Grant, I thought. Then Grant twisted around and his lovely green eyes narrowed and fired burning arrows directly at Travis. So maybe it wasn't so nice.

"Everybody just shut the hell up!" Grant screamed.

And they did. I looked at the faces surrounding us. Most of them wore smirks, the expression learned on playgrounds everywhere. Jeez, what a way to make a newcomer feel welcome. I made nasty faces back at all of them.

Grant took a moment staring at his teed ball, breathing deeply. Then he made a perfectly gorgeous swing, his ball sailing straight as a bullet for the pin. And it kept sailing, over the flag, beyond the green, and into the sand bunker 10 yards behind it.

The crowd at the green voiced its disappointment, sounding more sympathetic than the drunken clowns around the tee box. Maybe the loudmouths had been subdued by Grant's powerful shot. I didn't care enough to find out, because I couldn't take my eyes off Grant. He dropped his head, grimaced, and nonchalantly picked up his tee. It was all I could do not to rush to his side and hug him. Yeah, like that would help. I busied myself with handing Tom his chosen club and giving him his own personal pep talk.

Everyone watched in hopeful amazement as Tom's shot went straight, looking good for 160 yards. Then it landed short and rolled to a stop 12 feet from the pin. Nevertheless, the crowd gave him a raucous ovation, clearly as surprised as he was for coming so close.

"Great shot, Mr. Vanlandingham," I said loudly, using his last name to show due respect in front of his homies.

Then Travis came up, swinging his iron lightly back and forth. He teed his ball, pushed his glasses back on his nose as he looked down the fairway, and said, "Let's get this over with. We're holding people up here."

Several in the gallery gave him shouts of encouragement, more than one announcing that they had bet on him.

"I want that free round of golf, buddy. Get it in the hole!"

"Do it, Tiger! You da man."

"Come on, Hippie. Use your karma."

People laughed until Travis put his hand out in a "settle down" gesture, smiling shyly as he did so. He wiggled his skinny, jeans-clad butt and took his swing.

There was a barely audible *tick* as the sweet spot of the club head found the ball. The crowd began chanting in unison, "In the hole! In the hole! In the hole!"

I was more accustomed to seeing the pins than most others around us. From this distance, with the wind blowing, it was hard for them to follow the ball's roll towards the hole. But I knew it was going in.

"Sweet, Trav," I told him.

The crowd around the green burst into an outrageous uproar that travelled down the length of the fairway. My players rushed in to congratulate him and shield poor Travis from the overwhelming hordes that surrounded him. Through the huddle, I could see that Grant was the first to shake his hand and give him a brusk buddy-thump on the shoulder.

Jake, standing next to me, said, "Wow. Good ol' Travis. Couldn't have happened to a nicer guy."

"Yeah, I know. I'm happy for him. He's really going to appreciate the free golf."

"Yep. I guess this means we'll be seeing him out here all the time, doesn't it?" He smiled at me. When I didn't respond, he waggled his eyebrows, still staring at me.

"What are you getting at, Jake?" I asked.

Before I got an answer Grant approached us, remaining slightly off to the side.

Jake said, "Hell of a shot, Mr. Garner." With his usual good-natured candor he added, "A little less club and it would've caught the flag."

Grant huffed a humble laugh. "Thanks."

Jake left us. Grant looked at the ground and said, "Sorry, Lainey."

"What are you talking about? Don't be sorry to me. That you didn't make a hole-in-one? They don't happen every day, you know. Travis got lucky."

He shook his head and looked away.

"I'm sorry I choked. I let 'em get to me."

"Well, with good reason," I asserted. "They were so mean!"

He laughed. "I'd kiss you right now, Wild Thing, if there weren't so many people watching."

Tom called to us then, "Let's get going. We want a chance to find Buzz's ball."

We didn't find it. Buzz and Tom agreed to waive the 5-minute-search allotment, due to the build-up of teams waiting behind us. They took a drop, chipped, and putted out. Travis, apparently unruffled by his new-found fame and fortune, lobbed Grant's ball out of the bunker and onto the green. Grant easily putted it in for a par. Rover's Dream Team won the hole and Tom handed Grant the $10.

It was close to four when we finished our round and commandeered golf carts back to the pro shop. The score-board showed the low score was going to "The Dudes," two guys I'd never seen before who wore matching black slacks and gold polos. Although our teams didn't win any prize money, the Pork Bellies didn't do too badly. It was announced that Buzz Inskeep had brought in the most pledges, winning himself a huge combo basket full of merchants' donated goodies. And like Travis had promised his homies if he'd won a basket, Buzz said he'd share it with the muni gang.

I saw Tom collecting payoffs from more than one of the other players. He tried to pay me a tip but I refused.

"Mr. Vanlandingham... Tom... it was a real pleasure carrying your bag. I had fun."

"Ms. Tidwell... Lainey... this was the most fun I've had in years. I'm going to have to win some more bets to be able to do it again soon," he said with a wink.

Buzz said, "And it was an honor to play with you two lads." Everybody was shaking everybody else's hands. "Very challenging. But you have to admit, we gave you a run for your money."

Grant agreed. "Yes, sir. We may have outscored you, but I'm out $20 on the match play. Great game."

"And you, young man," Buzz said to Travis, "Congratulations again. I'm just glad I was there to see it."

"Thank you. Hey. Let's play sometime out at the muni. You and Tom can make your hole-in-one out there and I'd like to be around to see that."

"You betcha, kid," Tom said, winking again. I think he'd had a few too many beers. It had been a long day.

We stuck around long enough to watch the tournament honchos give Travis his certificate for a free season, which he received in typical, humble style. When someone yelled out, "Way to go, Tiger!" he casually said, "No relation. I'm taller."

Then Grant and I headed for the car.

My attempts at small talk as Grant drove us home got nowhere. He was sullen and kept his eyes on the road. I finally hit on a subject I thought he couldn't resist.

"Hey, you know what? I'm starving."

Silence.

"Let's go get cleaned up and have a nice dinner at Rosaria's."

Still nothing.

"It's good and small, familiar, friendly, probably won't see anyone from the Bluffs there. My treat," I coaxed.

He slowly smiled, and without looking at me said, "Okay. We can go to Rosaria's. But you're not paying."

I didn't say anything for a minute, also keeping my eyes on the road.

Then, softly, I said, "Am too."

Grant reached for my hand, brought it to his mouth for a sweet kiss, and chuckled.

CHAPTER 23

GRANT ORDERED AN expensive red wine that was really tasty. I decided that was probably not how you're supposed to describe a good wine, so I just said, "Yum!" and carefully set my glass back down on the white table cloth.

He was looking through the lace curtains at Rover, who was standing in the driver's seat of the car parked at the curb. The car window was down and Rover was half out of it, seeming to be thoroughly entertained watching the passing cars and pedestrians.

"He doesn't ever jump out?" Grant asked.

"Not in town. He does at the resort, but never leaves the parking lot. Here, I think he's afraid he might miss something if he wanders off."

Grant kept his eyes on the rascally mutt wagging contentedly from his post on the soft leather armrest. "He does look pretty happy," he said.

The background violin music and muted conversations of other diners in the small room were relaxing me into a mellow mood. I took another sip of wine as I read the menu.

"Are you going to have the crab ravioli?" I asked. "Because if you do, I'll have something else and then you can give me a bite, and I'll give you a bite of whatever I have. I'm thinking of the special. What did Stephanie call it? Spazzy-tino with pepperoni? Is that like a pizza?"

Grant turned his gaze from the window to his menu.

"*Spezzatino di pollo con peperoni.* Chicken in garlic wine sauce with sweet peppers," he said without looking up.

"Sounds good when you say it. Do me a favor... order for me and save me from further embarrassment," I said, and mopped a piece of bread through the olive oil, taking a big bite as soon as I saw Stephanie heading towards our table.

He handed her the menus and gave our order. When she was gone, he finally faced me.

"Speaking of embarrassment, I want to apologize for being such an ass today. I was way out of line." He waited for me to set my bread crust on the plate, then he put his hand around mine. "I'm sorry, Lainey."

He was in such obvious misery that I had to look away.

Before he could continue, I said, "I told you, there's no need to apologize. So? You got a little hot when a bunch of drunks mouthed off to you. So what? That was totally uncool that they did that. They should know better than to catcall a golfer when he's going through his pre-shot routine. I'm embarrassed for *them.*"

I realized I'd taken my hand out of Grant's and was using it, plus the one previously attached to my wine glass, to express

216

my irritation. I put them both in my lap and tried to let the music bring me back to that mellow place.

"Lainey, I'm not talking about the gallery." He picked up his glass and turned to the window again. After a moment, he took a sip and set it down. His eyes connected with mine and he continued. "Today was supposed to be fun for you, and I ruined it..."

"No, you didn't," I argued.

"Let me finish. I ruined it by showing off like an idiot, getting all cocky and competitive, trying to make out like I was so much better than Travis and the rest of them."

Now Grant was talking with *his* hands.

"I don't know what got into me," he said, clasping his fingers together on the table and focusing on them. I waited. "I think I'm just feeling really out of place here."

I racked my brain for something I could say to make it all better for him. Finding nothing, I stalled by watching Stephanie and Rosaria wind through the tables, both in friendly conversations with customers they knew. Then I turned to look out the window. A group of teenagers walked by, playfully messing around with each other. One boy who was walking backwards and laughing I recognized as a punky, but harmless, kid from my neighborhood. They were heading for the Safeway parking lot, I thought, to hang out and hope for friends with cars to happen by. As I watched them, Rover let out a cheerful bark and a horn honked. It was Jessica, on her way home from the bar and saying hi to my dog.

Something occurred to me.

"Grant, remember at Gail and Stewart's Fourth of July party, when you told me that you thought Eden Beach was too 'fuzzy' for you? I'm guessing you didn't mean that as in warm and fuzzy."

He gave a half laugh. "No, not warm and fuzzy. Just fuzzy, as in... indistinct, like I can't quite make out what it is."

"But you know it isn't you."

"Yes, I think that's what I'm trying to say."

We drank some more wine.

After a moment, he leaned forward suddenly and said, "But damn, Lainey. I really thought I could do it. I thought I was ready."

"Ready for what? For Eden Beach? Or for me?"

He drew his lips in, biting down hard as if to keep the answer from escaping.

I had only a second to worry about what that meant, because Stephanie was there with our plates. She set them down with a lengthy, animated discourse on each item, a trait she must've acquired from Rosaria.

When she finally finished, I said, "Thank you," and picked up my fork.

The next thing I heard was, "Don't you dare dig into that before you hear my answer."

I put down my fork. I was afraid to look at him. But I did, and found Grant's lovely green eyes crinkling a smile that I needed more than I needed the spazzy-tino.

"I am *so* ready for you in my life, Lainey," he said with such emotion that I found myself tearing up. "I can't imagine how I've gone this long without you. But now that I do have you... and I mean that as in two people having each other... I want you with me always. I love you, Lainey."

He disengaged his eyes from mine and forked a ravioli.

"Now eat your *spezzatino*."

We ate, and talked, and laughed, both of us ignoring the 10-ton commuter plane in the room, the miles between us. When the last of the wine was poured and our desserts served, things got quiet again. Grant cleared his throat. The bite of cherry *croste* in my mouth was suddenly difficult to swallow and I thought I heard a drum roll.

"Lainey, come to Seattle. Come live with me."

My life flashed before my eyes. But not my past life. My future life, and I'm not even sure if it wasn't someone else's future life. A lush condo overlooking Pioneer Square, the blue waters of Puget Sound in the background, a silver tray laden with bagels and a pitcher of coffee next to a canopied king size bed with a scruffy dog lying on top of a soft, fluffy, white comforter... wait, what?

"Grant, I can't. Not that I don't think I could live with you. I think I could. I mean I think I love you too. Being with you makes me happier than I thought possible, and living together sounds wonderful."

"Then move in with me, Lainey. Please. You'll love Seattle." His voice trailed off into almost a whisper.

"Not as much as I love it here, and not as much as you'd hate leaving there... I mean not as much as you'd love leaving here... I mean me leaving here. Oh, crap."

Get a grip, Tidwell. Deep breath. Start over.

"Grant, you're sweet to ask. But it just won't work."

He let out his breath, still looking me straight in the eye, and nodded.

"I know. You're right," he said. "It would never work out. We're from different planets. I guess I'm just not cut out for this kind of thing." He held out his hand to indicate the scene outside. A guy had stopped his beat-up truck in the middle of the street and was yelling a friendly conversation with another guy passing by carrying a crab pot and a bucket.

"Actually," he continued, "it was you who made me realize that I do fit in Seattle, I do appreciate its heart and soul.

"And you in Seattle... I can't even imagine you feeling comfortable walking down the city sidewalks." He shook his head. "You'd never get used to following Rover around with a poop-bag everywhere you went."

My laugh was so loud it startled other diners.

Grant drank some wine and smiled at me over the rim of his glass. I returned the gesture.

"You know," I said, "for a minute there I thought you were serious."

He shrugged. "It was worth a shot. And admit it, it sounded good for that minute. Didn't it?"

"Yes, it did." I sighed heavily enough to get wary looks from the diners again. "Can I still come for a visit?"

"You'd better. I promised to show you the raunchiest joints in town, didn't I?"

"Yep. Can't wait for that." I thought a moment. "You don't have a white comforter, do you?"

"On my bed? Uh, no. It's navy, I think. Plaid."

"Okay, good," I said. "How about late fall? It will be easier then for me to take a longer break from the resort. I'd be able to stay longer. That is, if you want me to."

"I'm pretty sure I'm going to want you to," he said, his eyes doing their best to rattle what was left of my determined resolve. "But there's one thing you absolutely have to do first."

220

When his crinkly eyes changed from amorous to adamant, I got worried.

"What?"

He leaned in and whispered, "Let everyone at the Singing Bluffs Resort know that you, Lainey Tidwell, are the best freaking golf caddie they've ever known."

I nodded once and said, "I can do that."

We sat back and looked at each other without speaking. I was the first to crack.

"Now what do we do?"

He shrugged, looked around the room, then back at me.

"I don't know. Finish up here and go back to your place for break-up sex?"

"Sounds good. Let's go."

CHAPTER 24

FOR THE FIRST time, I bagged for a double loop during the week. Twice. And on the other days I had players who needed a lot of handholding. I seemed to have energy to burn, and I didn't want any extra time that allowed my mind to wander. By Sunday, I was ready to veg out. When the sun was high enough to hit my front porch, I took a cup of coffee and sat outside with Rover. There was a dry, light wind from the east and streaks of cirrus clouds were making interesting shapes across the bright sky. It was unusually warm, and it made me feel like there was something cosmically weird going on. Or weirdly cosmic. What do I know? I'm surprised that the cloud names I learned in 6th grade science stayed with me.

It was a good time to get out my cell phone and call my folks. I hadn't been up to talking to them on the previous Sunday, and I owed it to my mom to tell her that I would be single for a while yet.

"Hello, Sweetheart." It was my dad's voice.

"Dad! What are you doing answering the phone?"

"We've got this new phone with an ID doohickey. Hell of a thing. I knew it was you," he said proudly, as if he'd invented it himself.

"Cool. Now there's nothing getting past you, Dad."

We chatted about the weather, the Giants, and Rover for all of sixty seconds – a record for Dad – then he said, "I'll get your mother."

"Lainey, how nice. How's everything?" she said when she picked up.

"Everything is great. I'm sitting outside and it's going to be a beautiful day. Dad says it's nice there, too."

"Yeah, we're probably going to work out in the yard. Nothing exciting. But how about you? Are you doing anything special with some friends? I hope you don't have to go to the golf course today."

"No, I'm not working today. It's been a long week. I'm going to spend the day by myself, just me and Rover, tooling around."

"Where's your friend, Jessica? And what about your boyfriend? The last time we talked you said Grant was coming down to see you. Did you two get some time together?"

"Jess is busy today. And about Grant, Mom. I... *we* decided to relax our relationship for the time being."

"Relax your relationship? What's that mean? I assumed you were having sex with him – how much more relaxed can you get?"

"*Mom!*"

"Well, I'm sorry, Lainey. I'm just trying to understand. Tell me what's wrong."

So I told her. I explained his reluctance to live in Eden Beach, and my reluctance to leave it. As always, Mom grasped the big picture while I was still trying to find the right words.

"You both should be proud of yourselves for being reasonable about it. Especially since it's obvious how much you care for each other. I know it's not easy, Sweetie."

"No, I guess not. But it's been a week, and we've talked on the phone a few times. Like friends. I'm actually doing okay. That's what's kinda weird. I'm not crying my heart out or anything. You'd be surprised, Mom."

"No. No, Lainey, I'm not surprised at anything coming from you. You always find your own way, and I know you're happy doing it. That's all that matters to your dad and me. Say, why don't you splurge and take a little time off from your work? Break your routine up a little?"

"It's the middle of the high season! The resort has reservations booked up solid. They'd have a fit if I left."

"Oh, I'm sure they can get by without you for a few days. And won't they always need good caddies? So you'll be right back to work when you're good and ready."

Mom's version of resort management was kinda skewed, but she was right about one thing. They needed caddies and would always give work to the good ones. And their favorites in that regard were those who hadn't caused any riffs. So far, my record was clean.

"I'll think about it, Mom."

IT WAS ANOTHER glorious day for the beach, and all of the easy-access places were crawling with people. Not that I

224

disliked the crowds, because from what I could see from the parking lots they all seemed to be minding their manners and sharing nicely. I spoke to a few people I knew, but declined to join them. What I wanted was something more remote. A place where I could sit and listen to the ocean and the birds, where Rover could wander on his own and I wouldn't have to worry about him bothering anyone, where I could enjoy the scenery without interruption.

The place that came to mind was a few miles out of town, a little-used viewpoint on a bluff covered with Scotch broom and blackberries. If you knew how to negotiate the trail, you could get to where it opened up on a sand dune. A soft slide to the bottom (or *on* your bottom, is more like it) and you found yourself in a secluded shorebird paradise. Rover and I had made our way there once before. We agreed that the downhill ride was fun but the climb back up was a killer.

I laughed out loud when I saw Gail's Mustang at the trailhead. I'd been looking for solitude, but there was nobody's company I'd enjoy more at that moment. We hiked in and stopped at the top of the dune to see Gail and Angel sitting peacefully in the dry sand, not twenty feet from a flock of feeding sanderlings. Rover immediately tore down the dune, alerted Angel, and they both did their best to rid the shore of the birds.

I took off my shoes and slid down the hill. "Well, so much for your quiet commune with nature," I said. "Sorry we interrupted."

"No, it's perfect. I'm glad you're here. Watch." She nodded in the direction that the dogs had gone. "Angel's been chasing those birds since we got here. They're diverted for a minute, they take a little excursion out over the ocean, then they come right back to that spot. Where they wanted to be all along."

I sat down and we watched Angel and Rover run at the birds. The flock took flight in a rolling formation above the waves, circled around and landed back where they started.

The dogs gave it a couple more tries, then turned towards the creek for a drink. The sanderlings settled back in front of us and continued their feeding.

Gail smiled at me. "Wouldn't you know that you and I would both have the same idea today, coming here? Trying to get away from it all?"

"Sort of, I guess. Weird weather, huh? It seemed like the right day to be here."

"Beats working at the farm. Travis is helping Stewie repair some old fencing and I had to leave. When those two work together the bullshit gets deep fast. It's amazing they get anything accomplished."

"Sounds fun. Is Travis good at that sort of stuff?"

"Oh, yeah," she said, nodding. "He's a good kid."

Standing up, she said, "Well, we're about ready to get back. So I'll leave you to yourself."

"Stay and talk for a while, if you can. We haven't had a chance since your party on the Fourth. That was great, by the way. Thanks for inviting me. And Grant."

She sat down again and got comfortable. "What's bothering you, kiddo?"

I faked a look of confusion before asking, "What gave me away?"

"You're sighing a bit more than usual."

"I am?"

"Just a little. But you can't help it. You're twenty-four, you're female, you're befuddled. Been there."

At that we both burst into giggles. We went a little nuts. Every time we'd almost get a grip on ourselves, one of us would lose it and we'd get going again. I hadn't laughed that hard in a long time.

When we finally ran out of gas, Gail said, "Oh, that was great. So, tell me. What's not working out?"

I took a deep breath, and sighed. "Grant doesn't want to live here. It's too small. He asked me to move in with him."

"Downtown Seattle, right? Whew. I can just see you in the city, struttin' your stuff, wearing high-fashion, some bling, spiked heels."

"Yeah, right."

"What did you tell him?"

"I thought about it. I really did. And for once in my life, I was dead certain about the answer." I let loose of the hug I had around my bent knees, sat up straight and turned to Gail. "I *love* Eden. It took me a while to realize that. I mean, face it. It's got more than its share of crackpots. But people here are who they are – good, bad, or ugly. There isn't any of the pretentiousness that I've seen in big cities. I like that."

"What about the golf course?" Gail asked.

"Oh, you're right. There's *plenty* of pretentiousness there." I hugged my knees again.

"No. I mean what are you going to do about caddying?" She laughed. "Would you just give yourself a break? You're over-thinking this."

"Oh, caddying. Yeah, I'm sticking through the winter. Finally, I've stumbled into something that suits me. I'm fairly good at it, I can make a decent living, and no one comes unglued if my hair isn't perfect or I accidently burp out loud."

"And you love it." She gave me that knowing, reassuring smile, the one I always hear in my mother's voice on Sunday phone calls.

"I do love it. Do you think it will last? Can I really make a go of this?"

"Of course. You probably need to step back from everything for a bit. Relax. My advice, kiddo, is to go with your gut." She stood up and dusted off her behind. "Lainey, for you, things always seem to land in the right place eventually."

She whistled for Angel, touched my shoulder with a gentle pat of her hand, and said, "Now for that fucking climb back to the car."

AFTER LEAVING THE beach, I stopped at the post office on my way home. It had been days since I'd checked my box, but I wasn't expecting anything. I stood over the trash barrel and flicked the junk mail into it one by one. The last piece in the stack was a postcard, the photo showing a fancy lodge with a background of bright blue sky and smooth, green fairways. The small, cramped handwriting on the back was Tiny Sue's.

It read, "Hey Lainey, how's my favorite mouthy broad? I hope life in Eden isn't hell. This season's been phenomenal – too much to say on a card. I told you I'd be in Sun River. Well, it's happening. Where will you be next week? It's only a day's drive from Eden. Come share the joy, even if only for a short stay. I don't have your cell #, so call me."

She'd added her cell phone number and wrote on the edge of the card, "POWER TO THE SHORT GRRLS!"

I climbed back into the Jeep and when I turned the engine on, the oldies channel was playing Jimmy Buffett's "Cheeseburger in Paradise." I started singing along as I drove, and Rover looked at me with his head cocked. By the time Jimmy and I got to "*I like mine with lettuce and tomato,*" Rover was in sync. With the added effect of his happy barks out the open window, our concert drew rave reviews from the people we passed.

Predictably, at the end of the song I said, "I'm hungry. You know what? I'm going to treat myself to lunch at the Garden."

Rover wagged agreeably.

"Then, whaddaya say we go home and get ready for a Road Trip?"